SLUGGER

Stories that hit you in the mouth

Vol. 1

Edited by Sam Logan & Arwyn Sherman

Cover Art by Kae Ranck

Interior Layout & Format by Leo Otherland

Editors' Note

We are stoked to introduce you to SLUGGER Vol. 1! Our first submission call opened June 15th and closed July 15th, 2025. We had no idea what to expect, but y'all showed up! We received over 400 submissions and were absolutely thrilled with the response. The quality and originality of the stories were so refreshing. We sincerely thank all the writers who submitted their work and trusted us with the review and publishing process.

This first volume features 10 original short stories. While horror is central to all of them, there is a vast mix of how that manifests—folk, sci-fi, pre-apocalyptic noir, weird, supernatural, monsters, cosmic, thriller, and of course, the body. We love all these stories, and we know you will too.

In keeping with the punk ethos that generated SLUGGER's inception, we also have three nonfiction pieces that relate to music in some way in the "Sound Trails" section.

Famous last words of an indie publisher—we will be around for a long time, and we hope you join us for the ride.

Cheers,
Sam and Arwyn
October 2025

Contents

Art by Emma Fujikawa

A Cat Walked Across the Keyboard

By
Michael Bettendorf

It's weird being in two places at once. My body sits reclined at my desk, a flesh-heap hooked up to my hardware, while my avatar wades through the digital void of the net. I bypass corporate asset protection firewalls and undercover CopBots as a crowd of users tries to size me up and sniff out what I'm holding while I navigate the Pathway, dressed in a workaday leather jacket and jeans.

A notification appears in my feed.

< Running late. Be there soon. >

We could have done this off-net, away from the strobing lights and pounding audio that feels like I'm getting clocked in the head with every line of code running in the background. It'd be easier that way. Moving illegal software is stressful enough without the added fanfare.

But life on the net is what people live for. Less social pressure. More anonymity and freedom to do the kind of shit we do. The net is easier, too. Why mess with traffic or risk getting roughed up when you can do everything from home?

The idea of the future is what people love about life on the net. The spectacle of the neon rain soaking the artificial nighttime. Fixing your avatar just right so you can be who you want to be at all times. Be who you really are.

And if getting digitally pummeled is what it takes to help erase my mistakes, then I'll put up my dukes and take a few on the cheek because illegal doesn't mean illegitimate. People deserve to have the software I sling at the rate I'm selling it. It's all about access. My software gives people access to optimize their gear. No corporate price-jacks. No software/hardware incompatibilities. The stuff people wouldn't need if it weren't for the arbitrary data caps and bandwidth throttling. But if the corporations won't play fair, why should we? We don't owe them anything.

I round the corner to our meeting spot. A dime-a-dozen digital café. A hub for new users to get their feet wet on the net. A place for wannabe hackers. Neopunks flashing their shit, trying to look tough. Important. These places are information playgrounds for serious folks. Easy pickings. Fucking dopes wouldn't last a minute on the Pathways I used to frequent.

The buyer still hasn't shown and for the briefest moment—a hummingbird whisper—I consider I'm being set up. Could be that they're just spooked. First time buyer, maybe. Or perhaps, distracted by the ads on the way here, tantalized by what the net markets have to offer, they blew through their cash. Only takes one click.

I consider taking a seat as planned, sip on automated espresso. Instead, I stroll past the café just in case, and head for a dive bar off the beaten Pathway. No one follows. It's just me and the neon breeze.

I message the buyer, < Café felt off. Sending you the address to a bar. Keep to the Pathway on the address and you'll be fine. >

< nb nb. >

Something about the reply begins to jostle a memory loose, but I can't quite place it. *Nb*. I figure they meant *np, no problem*. A typo. Who knows? I alter the code as I walk. Just a line here or there, tweaking the right bits so I end up on the Pathway I want to be on. The ones you have to know about in order to find. It isn't that it's tough to navigate. It's more about the privilege of being privy to the info. A wrong line of code isn't the end of the world. It's like walking down the wrong street off-net. You may get lost. No problem. Unless you end up in the wrong kind of neighborhood, then you might have many problems.

That's how this place feels, like a wrong turn.

It's purposeful though. A warning to those who wander in by accident: *Turn around*. But I'm not here by accident. I meander toward a vending machine beside the front entrance. Prices haven't changed. Options haven't changed. I consider punching the well-worn button B9, my favorite digital hallucinogen, but instead I tap A4 and watch a bag of chips drop from its coiled dispenser rack. Nostalgia will be my drug of choice tonight. Have to maintain a clear head while making deals these days. Keeps me straight. Keeps me breathing.

I sit at an empty barstool and stare at a warped version of myself in the mirror behind the bar, lined with bottles programmed so well you'd think they're real, especially if your hardware is good enough. I order a scotch. Then a water. They taste how I remember them. I think about all the time spent here in my twenties, when I was fucked up both on and off-net. I existed in a digital haze. Gaps in my memory so big a train could run through them. Wish I could I say I didn't miss it, not the time spent here, but the fluidity of youth. When the ticking clock telling you to make something of yourself seemed to run in slow-motion. Maybe I was just moving too fast to notice.

Time is weird on the net. Measured in megabits per second. Users are all manifestations of data being thrust here and there and it feels seamless—until it doesn't. That's how I know something is off. I feel the lag. It starts as a subtle pull. There's another message from the buyer, but it's gibberish, like a cat walked across the keyboard. The glinting liquor bottles twist and blur into kaleidoscopic lines. Then the lag shifts from subtle and inconvenient to overwhelmingly slow and paralyzing.

A barrage of pings come through my audio feed, alerts from the bot watching my off-net security system.

The feeling is like I've walked into a room, and the moment I crossed the threshold, I've suddenly forgotten where I am and where I came from. That's what improperly disconnecting from the net is like. A confusing cacophony of neural static as my two worlds compile and run into one another again.

Someone is screaming at me, but my senses are dull and it sounds like it's coming from underwater. Synaptic lag. I look around, vision blurry, and almost run my kill switch program—corrupting all my gear. Software. Hardware. Everything. A hard reboot, but evidence gone.

I focus and see an old friend, Trevor, dragging a body through the doorway.

"You've got to help me," he says and kicks the door shut.

The deadbolt, still in the locked position, has ripped apart the catch and doorjamb. The door creeps open to the dark hallway. My first instinct isn't to help, but to call Trevor a piece of shit. Tell him to leave. Call nine-one-one. His problems weren't my problems any longer. That ended a long time ago, just like our friendship did when I quit dealing narcotics. Trevor stopped hanging around after I got clean. When I quit selling to him. Cutting him deals. Funny how that works.

"I don't have to do anything, Trevor."

His name lingers in the air, and I consider that I've never met anyone named Trevor who didn't have trouble clinging to them like flies on shit. In this case, trouble's a mid-twenties blonde. Trevor grips her under the shoulders and lugs her farther into my apartment. Her shoes slide across the floor, leaving a small trail of gravel and grime for me to sweep later.

"Do it for her," he says, knowing goddamn well the weight of the look he shoots me. The way he emphasizes the word *her*. The memories it trudges up. The mistakes.

"Shut the fucking door and help me," I say.

A quick assessment of her clothes tells me she was ready for a night out. Trevor's moving impossibly fast, but moments like these tend to pull time like taffy, stretching it thin until you can see through it. Her eyelids flutter like a dreaming dog's. The unnatural pink hue of her irises tells me she's either wearing contacts or she's augmented. But knowing Trevor's type, she's geared up.

I kneel and check her airways. She's not seizing, but her eyes keep dancing. I yell at him to grab *the bag*. He knows the one. Narcan. Epinephrine. The kind of stuff I needed before I sold software. The reason I deal only in software now.

"She's goddamn overdosing, man. Get it together."

I rotate her slightly and notice she's burning up, but it's localized to her head and neck. She's got a single socket implant behind one ear. A neural jack behind the other. I turn to Trevor, his eyes all bloodshot and panicked. He's shaking his head *no* because she's not overdosing.

"She's overclocking."

And there's the slightest grin on his face. Accidental. Nerves betraying him. Some information I'm not privy to, but he seems to be amused. The slimy fucker.

I don't have time to ask questions. Instead, I tell Trevor to grab all of the icepacks from the freezer and place them around her head, while I grab my interface cables. I connect to her neural link and am bathed in neon.

Navigating her BIOS should be easier than this, but this isn't the first time she's overclocked. Her boot data has been corrupted, scarred, and there's static everywhere along the Pathway, making it difficult to traverse. She'll need a true tech to fix her right. Her augment system is fucked, but if I can manually reduce her settings back to normal processing levels, I might be able to keep her hardware from frying her brain or giving her permanent nerve damage. Won't save her from eventual surgeries, but should be a hell of a lot cheaper. Hopefully less painful, but probably not.

The typical Pathway is blocked, encrypted in a series of randomized loops that are programmed to maximize the effects for a set duration before timing out. I recognize it, because I wrote it. She's overclocking on my shit.

"Fuck."

The program is meant to maximize system processing, and performance. Lets you run all sorts of programs you shouldn't be able to do. Ignore bandwidth throttling. But it's bypassing the intended Pathway, linked so the surges are hitting her hardware receptors for an on-net high of a lifetime. Misuse of a good thing.

This is the kind of thing Trevor would abuse. Always pushing things. New highs were only new for so long, but I never sold him software.

I move quick, taking a back channel, until I'm finally able to restore her hardware to default settings. I stick around and keep an eye on her processing temps.

While I wait, I poke around in her memory. I shouldn't, but I have to know where she got my shit. Was it Trevor or coincidence? Residual messages float around in here. Pieces of conversations she's had with a familiar user. The handle and last IP match the user I was supposed to meet at the café before I was yanked from the net. The last thing he said before I hooked up my interface cables. *I'll keep her cool, no biggie, no biggie*—the user's shorthand *nb*. *Nb*. Trevor's look. The *got you* smirk. He knew it was my program. He knew I'd never sell to him if I knew what he was doing with it.

The blonde's temps are stable. There's nothing else I can do, but disconnect and let her ride it out and hope the neurological damage doesn't leave her with chronic pain or worse, but I won't hold my breath. He let her run the program for far too long. Too many times. Well, no more.

The plan was to beat Trevor's ass when my mind returned to reality, but he's gone, along with a myriad of loose microchips and hard drives from my desk. I disconnect the interface cables linking me to the girl. The floor is slicked with sweat as she shakes, coming down hard. Her neon pink irises fade to a beautiful, natural hazel as her augment system crashes. She won't remember anything clearly, her memories corrupted by carelessness. Hers and mine.

I move her to the couch and place a blanket over her. I replace the icepacks with cold ones, wrapped in dishrags, and occasionally monitor her breathing.

My hardware *dings*, a message from the user— Trevor—asking me if she made it. Playing with me now.

I contemplate my move. Trevor thinks he's got me. Can't go to authorities about the gear he boosted, even if I wanted to, given it'd be coded as digital paraphernalia. The girl was ODing on my software. Probably thinks I'll jump on the deal to recoup my losses. Then what, Trevor? Going to set me up? Get me busted so I'm off the market. Then use the gear he stole to take my place?

< C'mon man. No hard feelings. Deal still on? >

I've told him no a thousand times. I'm not selling to him again. Quitting him wasn't enough though. It doesn't matter what I'm selling, people will find a way to drown in the neon rain. And the Trevors of the net will be there to hold their heads under. Life on the net is living in desperation, treading in the digital sea. Addiction. Users, all. I've gotta be done for good—with everything. We all sell shit. Products. Drugs. Our names. A good time. No ethical consumption under capitalism. Maybe it's a bad excuse, but I did it to keep the fucking lights on. Trevor? It was for control. To have power over people's habits.

He can't have that kind of power any longer. I'm going to have to boost it from him.

And to do so, I reply *yes* and wait for Trevor to log on using my gear. I don't bother using spare interface cables. Instead, I log on to the net using a proxy user. There are messages from him asking where to meet.

< The café. Same Pathway as before. >

I need this to be public. Flashy. It's the only way to combat the noise of the net. People need to know I'm gone for good.

I guide my proxy using the command prompt, no need for graphical interfaces. I know these Pathways like the back of my hand. I wait for Trevor to sit before I remotely disable the firewall protections on my gear. He won't know what the nagging pings picking at his brain are. It doesn't take long—mere milliseconds—for scavengers and neo punks to catch wind of an easy haul. But on here? Time can be weird. A virus stripping you of all your data, unraveling your digital DNA, can feel excruciatingly slow.

< Smthng's wrrrrrong. i needd to baaaaiillll sryy >

The words appear on my monitor. A cat on his keyboard.

The Pathway is lagging due to the high traffic of users watching this unfold. I wonder how many of them have been misusing my software.

And how many will stop?

I type *nb*. *nb* and initiate the kill switch program, forever trapping Trevor in two places at once. Thrust into a state of constant synaptic lag. His thoughts stretched and pulled thin to where he can see through them, but they'll never snap. They'll pull and pull, unraveling his mind until he rots, a flesh-heap at his desk.

Eventually, I sweep the trail of grit and grime from the floor and wait for the blonde to wake up, taking care of Trevor's mess one last time.

Michael Bettendorf (he/him) is a multi-genre writer from the Midwest. His short fiction has appeared at Cosmic Horror Monthly, Mythaxis Magazine, the Drabblecast, and elsewhere. His debut experimental horror novel/gamebook "Trve Cvlt" was released by Tenebrous Press (Sept. 2024). Michael works in a high school library in Lincoln, NE. Find him on Bluesky @BeardedBetts and www.michaelbettendorfwrites.com.

Art by Kae Ranck

Hot Tub Hormone Xenotransfusion

By

L. Sanguine

"Fucking seagulls," says Mum, by way of greeting. She does an impression, a good one, of the gulls nesting in our neighbours' chimneys, so loud and sudden it makes me jump: "*EEEEE-ee-ee-ee!*"

"Jesus."

I ask her how the newspaper is while I wait for the kettle to boil for my instant coffee. She exhales wearily, starts to read the headlines aloud: *Adolescent gender service to be dissolved… Updated guidance causes division…*

I shake my head. That's enough.

"It's mad," I say, which is what I always say when I don't want to think about it. Instead, I focus on choosing a nice mug to cheer myself up. I ought to stop asking her about the paper.

She lifts her head to appraise my outfit. "You look nice today, honey. Are you going out?"

"Maybe."

"Well, there's another weather warning. More thunderstorms."

"For fuck's sake."

"Lightning struck a farmer's field out in Comber last night. Ten of his cows were killed."

"*Ten?*"

"He probably had them insured," she licks her index finger, turns the page, "But the smell of barbeque alone would haunt you, wouldn't it?"

I sit at the edge of my bed and bite and pull a hangnail 'til it bleeds. Dysphoria itches in the forefront of my mind: Binders haven't been fitting right recently. The thought that my tits might be getting *even bigger*, somehow, is fucking haunting me. Though I know it won't help, might even make it worse, I allow myself five minutes to check everything in the mirror. I pinch my hips (too curvy), flatten my shirt against my chest and scowl at my reflection. If only I could afford top surgery or lipo – but phalloplasty? That's a pipe dream. No pun intended.

I change my shirt, scrutinise, change back, scrutinise, change again. I have to open a window, despite the rain, because my bedroom smells like ripe bananas. It looks like most of the seagulls are gone for the day, probably finding shelter somewhere before the rain comes.

I message Ruby. I don't want to be alone right now.

Up to much?

Ruby, immediately, as if waiting for me: *Yep. It's ready. Come over.*

The blanket of clouds thickens, the sky darkens, but still no rain.

I bang on Ruby's door a little too hard. She's drawn my blood, snipped my hair, even asked me to miss a couple T shots so she could use the little 1ml ampules in her experiments. God knows what else she's been doing. I, the guilty nonbeliever, didn't think it would ever be *ready*. Not that I know much about pharmaceuticals, or alchemy, or whatever it is Ruby does. I was kind of just humouring her because she's my bestie.

She grins at the meal deals I brought with me. I figured she hadn't eaten yet. "They had egg and cress sandwiches," I tell her.

"Hell yeah, man," she says.

The stairs are covered in crumbs, dust bunnies, discarded plastic packages that crinkle under our feet. I'm used to Ruby's house looking like this; she's too busy with homebrew to clean anywhere but her "lab". When she first built her high-speed centrifuge—it took her weeks to source the parts— everyone told her it was going to, quite literally, blow up in her face. But it didn't.

Ruby dons her raggedy computer chair. She tears into her egg and cress sandwich, speaks through wet mouthfuls: "Okay, so, I just kind of need to prepare you for this."

"Sure," I say, patient as ever. Her bed frame creaks under my weight.

"You know how I said it was a pill?"

I nod. She looked into producing subcutaneous pellets, then suppositories, then got totally preoccupied with the idea of oral administration: A testosterone pill that doesn't get digested as a protein in the stomach, another viable alternative for trypanophobic trans men. Kind of impossible, I thought, but Ruby believed she could do it. She wanted to make it widely available, make a real name for herself. She even got some funding from a few crackpots online.

"Well, that wasn't working."

I'm not surprised. Talk about pipe dreams.

"So, it's *not* ready," I say.

"Oh, no, it's *ready*." The rain starts, thick droplets ramming up against her bedroom window. "It's just different. It's better. Absorbs through the skin, or… something like that."

My brow furrows.

Ruby waves a hand at me to dissipate my doubts. She takes another huge bite of her sandwich and chews just enough to speak: "*Not* like T-gel. You'll see."

Despite the bloodletting and the sacrifices of medication, I've never been invited into Ruby's lab before. I watch her open her attic door with a hook and climb up a creaky old ladder before she beckons me to follow.

I can make out the silhouette of… a blow-up swimming pool? I think.

"Okay," she whispers, "Ready?"

She flicks the lights on, and I realise it's a fucking hot tub. "How did you get a hot tub up here?"

She waves her hand again, irritated. "Why are you focusing on that? Look." She points to a little glass jar on a worktop. "They're bath salts!"

"What?"

"*Bath salts.*" She says it slowly, like speaking to a child.

I get closer and stare down at her mad-scientist bath salts. They're strawberry coloured, like something you'd buy from Lush, in a recycled onion relish jar. She has to be taking the piss.

"They're not literally salts," she clarifies.

"Right," is all I can think to say.

"That's just what I'm calling them. Sounds better, doesn't it?"

"Better than *what?*"

"You wouldn't understand if I told you, bro. As far as *you're* concerned, it's magic."

"Fair enough." I straighten, nervously pull at the front of my t-shirt. Thunder rumbles outside, rain batters the roof. I'm glad I got here before the storm really kicked off.

Ruby scoffs at my hesitation. "Like, seriously, this is so cool. You'll love it."

"Do I have to be naked?"

"Unless you want your clothes to get wet and, like, explode."

"*Explode?*"

"Joking."

Ruby turns her back to me so I can strip. I steel myself and tuck into a ball in the cold water of the hot tub, legs pressed against my chest to stop my tits from floating. I just hope this'll be over quickly,

whatever it is, and I *really* hope it isn't a prank. I look so stupid right now.

"So, what's the dosage, then? How often would I have to do this?" I ask, starting to shiver.

"Emmm…" Ruby continues to keep her eyes off my body as she scoops some of the little pinkish-red crystals into the tub with a measuring spoon. "I don't know how often, actually. I think you'll only have to do it once."

"*Once?*"

"We'll see," she says.

I trust Ruby, I really do, but I remember the time she caught a mouse just to inject it with an experimental breast growth serum, some kind of modified progesterone, and she never told me what happened to that mouse.

"You have to put your head under."

The water begins to heat rapidly. It's warm, really warm. Then it's hot, so hot I'm sweating. Blisteringly hot. It's starting to hurt. "I can't."

"No, you *have to.*"

I suck air in through my teeth. "Fine!" I dunk my head into the water, quickly, and I have every intention of lifting it back out before—

CRASH—I'm thrown around like a foetus in utero, toes curled in agony.

The pain is terrible, unique. My muscles stiffen like rigor mortis. I'm sure I'm dying. I fall deeper into the water, face-first, my legs still pressed up tight against my chest. My eyes sting, but I don't dare close them. I gasp in pain, get a lungful of chemicals and scorching-hot water. I'm being boiled like a lobster.

Like a super-rapid fourth-degree sunburn, great big bubbles form under my skin, fill with fluid, burst, and slough away; raw flesh is exposed to the salts, the chemicals, the searing heat. I seize and vomit into the tub. My eyes are cooking in their sockets, melting, I can't see. There's nothing but this unbearable—

Finally, I can't feel the pain anymore. I float, limp in the cooling water.

I'm not prepared to explain this to St. Peter.

But it's Ruby who grabs me by the hair and hoists me out of the water so I can breathe again. I take big gulps of air, gag and splutter. I realise my eyes are, actually, still there, and I open them.

"You're alive?"

Her face is covered in blood, her bangs wet, a wide gash on her forehead. I look up at the rain falling from a new hole in the roof.

My mouth waters. I barf again, all over myself: pink sludge. Tubby custard.

"What?" is all I can manage at first. I'm surprised I still have lips. I reach up to touch my face and it is smooth, waxy, free of blemish, like I've just had the world's most traumatic chemical peel.

"Dude, you got struck by lightning just now," says Ruby, "But you look great. I think it worked."

I look at my hands, turn them this way and that. My nails are long, healthy, stronger than ever; the little stumps and hangnail from two decades of biting are nowhere to be seen.

Ruby starts to drag me out of the tub and the water hisses around my ankles like it doesn't want me to leave. I fall to the floor like a wet and heavy fish, clamp my hands over my tits defensively—only to realise they aren't there.

They're *gone*. The ring of fat that made up my hips and ass is gone, too, all fallen away in the hot tub. I'm straight-up-and-down, hard and slender. I look back at the tub—the water is now a deep, impenetrable red. A foam of pink vomit sits on top.

Ruby has a wild grin on her face. "Isn't that insane?" She blinks blood from her eyes. "I can't believe it actually worked."

I ignore her admission, the obvious fact that I was a guinea pig (or, a mouse) for something she wasn't sure was safe, and I throw my arms around her, laughing.

She squeezes me joyously. "Look at you, look at you," she sings. Blood falls from her chin to my shoulder, trickles down my acne-free back. The sweet stench of it makes my head swim. My already empty stomach contracts again, forces me to pull away to dry heave. I hang my head between my knees, heart hammering in my (flat!) chest.

I'm eye-to-eye with my pussy, which seems to have survived the whole ordeal unscathed.

Ruby pushes her bloodied glasses up the bridge of her nose. "We missed a spot."

I heave again, managing this time to get up some slimy, yellow stomach lining that burns my throat.

"How do we do it?" I ask. I believe Ruby can do it, now.

She helps me back down to her room and tells me to sleep for as long as I want; she'll have it all figured out. I text Mum that I can't get home in the storm. I'm not sure how I'm going to explain this to her when I *do* go home, but I don't spend much time thinking about it. I pass out as soon as my head hits the pillow.

When I wake up, it's still raining. The streets are flooded.

Ruby spins around in her chair, smiles at me fondly like I'm a newborn baby. She cleaned and dressed her head wound while I was sleeping, but I can still smell the blood.

"Hungry?" she asks.

"I'm starving."

We order Chinese, Ruby's treat: Salt and chilli chicken, egg fried rice, spring rolls, sweet 'n' sour, prawn crackers, the whole shebang. I eat like I've never eaten before.

"So, about your cock," says Ruby.

"Yeah, my cock," says me, scarfing down the last of five spring rolls. I can't keep my greasy hands away from my gorgeous, sculpted chest.

"To be honest, I don't know how predictable the results are, but I think I know what was missing. I used a lot of, uh… *synthetic* T for that batch."

I try my best to understand. "You need a different kind of T? You're the hormone-monger. Can you get it online?"

Ruby wiggles her head from side to side. "Ehh… It'd be hard. I need it, like, straight from the source. If you know what I mean."

"Like, balls?"

Ruby laughs. "Not a bad idea. Plain old blood might do the trick, though."

"Are you serious?"

"I got a *liiiittle* bit last time," she admits. "A cis guy on a kink site who was really into vampires. Total chaser, too. He mailed it to me in a vial, and it took a while to get here, so… I'm not sure how good it was."

"Ew," I say. I blow my nose and more of the thick, pink sludge flies out into the tissue.

"Well," says Ruby, sweeping her hand at my new body. "It clearly worked. I think we just need better quality blood for your cock."

"Like, how much?"

Ruby pierces a hunk of sweet 'n' sour chicken. She shrugs. "As much as we can get."

I exhale, run my hand again over the hard chest. I want my dick. I want the complete set. Badly. But how do we get *as much blood as we can get?*

"You think anyone's going to die in this storm?" I ask her.

"Only if they're stupid enough to go outside."

The pavement is drowning. Plastic bottles rush past our feet in the stream of rainwater. Ruby wears her welly boots and a shiny yellow raincoat that makes her look like a little duck. She complains that she can't see because her glasses keep getting wet.

I catch glimpses of myself in puddles and car windows, marvelling at how handsome and strong I look. I could kiss myself. I smile—my teeth are glimmering, pearl-white, perfect.

"This could double as a youth serum," I tell Ruby. I poke at my canines, thinking Mum shouldn't have bothered paying for all that orthodontic work.

"You were already young."

"A health hack, then."

Ruby looks me up and down. I'm a little taller than her now, despite still hunching over like I'm trying to hide double-Ds. My socks are wet, my t-shirt soaking through, but I don't care. Not at all. She smiles proudly. "You do look healthy. Like a healthy young stallion."

"I feel, like, better than ever," I tell her. I laugh. My laughter is loud, clear, masculine.

Suddenly, Ruby *SHHH*s me and grabs my shoulder to stop me at a junction. "Look," she whispers.

Two young men on bikes, hooting and hollering, are coming down from the end of the street to our left. Ruby lifts her coat: Tubes, syringes, vials, little blue surgical gloves, a scalpel. She's looking at me expectantly.

With much sarcasm, I ask "Just grab them off the bikes, will I?"

But before Ruby has a chance to answer, before I have a chance to think, the boys are flying past us and I reach out (with a beautiful, muscular arm) to catch one of them like a bear sniping a salmon. He's heavy as he falls from his bike, my hand clasping his shirt collar. I almost go down with him.

"Shit!" Ruby cries, but I hold myself strong. Another euphoric laugh bubbles up out of my throat. I feel like a cat, slender and agile.

The boy claws and smacks at my arm. He wants me to let go of his shirt, I think, so I do. I shove him hard. His head smacks against the wet pavement—*thunk*—and he grunts, whines, blubbers like he's going to cry. The base of his skull is bleeding. He touches it, pulls his hand away, groans at the sight of the blood. He looks up at me, terrified. My mouth waters. I take him by the shirt and push, shove, throw him down again. Double *thunk*.

The other boy, Boy #2, does a U-turn on his bike and comes right at us, cursing and yelling. He sees Ruby and blurts "*TRANNY?*" like he can't believe it, like he's trying to warn someone, but I don't think his friend can hear him anymore.

I kick at the front wheel of his bike, and he goes over—"*FUCK*"—lands on his back.

Ruby is perched on the kerb, pushing wet hair out of her face. I turn to her as Boy #2 starts to pick himself up. "What now?"

She shrugs, gestures at Boy #2 like *you started it*. I stomp on him until he stops moving. Drool runs rivers down my chin, drips onto the flooded pavement: thick, pink, antacid, Pepto-Bismol.

Ruby starts her make-shift phlebotomy service on Boy #1, who is seemingly no longer conscious but continues to mumble and twitch. I stand over Boy #2 and take a look at what I was able to do to him. He's probably dead. The concave cavity of his chest is a mess of bumps and lumps, fresh red blood seeping through his football top.

I check to see if Ruby is watching—she isn't—and pull his top over his head. I take another moment to admire my work before I shove my face in the gaping blunt force wound. I gnaw at Boy #2's snapped ribs and mangled, squashed organs. I lap like a thirsty dog after a long walk. I catch his slick liver in my jaw, snap my head back to free it. He *stinks*.

When I reemerge from my stupor, Ruby is standing over me with three vials of blood in her hand. I shrink a little, ashamed, though my heart is pumping so fast it feels like it's going to pop. My pupils are dilated, my hands trembling with the excitement of it all.

"Need his balls?" I ask.

The tent in my jeans catches her eye, and she suddenly laughs.

"I guess not," she says.

L. Sanguine is a trans writer and artist from Belfast, N. Ireland. Butch by day and tboy by night, he prowls the local queer scene for inspiration. He enjoys writing short stories about disagreeable trans people for his friends.

Art by Emma Fujikawa

The Other Man

By
Kareem Miskel

Well, that's one way to end a rivalry.

Rose leaned against the headboard of her queen-sized bed. Her eyes drifted from her television over to Luke as he snoozed beside her. She could stream shitty sitcoms any time she wanted. Hulu and Netflix weren't going anywhere. But Luke would be gone no later than 8 p.m. on Sunday night.

Then it was back to pretending they were just coworkers. Contentious coworkers at that. It was exhausting but necessary. Solace Med Inc. had strict policies against their employees having romantic relationships, and she doubted they'd accept the excuse of "It's just physical."

More than that, she wasn't sure how true it was or how long it would stay that way. Three months in and she was already wondering what their children would look like. Would their first be a boy or a girl? Sandy-blond like his father or black-haired like her mother? Would their eyes be gray like his or brown like hers? With thoughts like that, things were bound to get serious sooner or later.

She ran her fingers through his thick locks. He was a beautiful man. Tall. Lean-muscled. There was even something attractive about his spattered freckles and comically large feet. How long before things got more serious? Before there were real feelings involved? She already loved his laugh, his grin, and his stupid jokes. She was already engrossed by his dull stories. And she already had trouble making it through the week without him. Without his scent on her skin. His breath on her neck. It was only a matter of time before they wanted more. What then?

That was Tomorrow-Rose's problem. Today-Rose was just enjoying the moment. She reached over and gently pressed her hand flat against his muscular back. A spark of lust flickered deep inside as the tip of her forefinger traced its way down his spine. She considered waking him up for round four but decided to let him sleep. She probably didn't have the energy for it anyway. And so, to the shitty sitcoms she looked.

A handsome, black baritone had just started asking if she was in good hands when her phone chimed. Rose snatched it up and read the text message.

MARIA: We're at Phantom's. Get out here!

Rose chuckled to herself. Maria was the definition of "work hard, play hard." She was all business in the office but when quitting time came on Friday she Yabba-Dabba-Dooed her way out with the rest of them. The clock read 10:24 p.m., and Maria was probably five or six sheets to the wind.

Rose hadn't told her about Luke. Maria was lower management. She got her the position and had warned her, "Don't make me look bad!" It was a great job, and Maria had put in five years. They were best friends but asking her to keep the Luke affair a secret could cost her everything. So, Rose's fingers danced across the screen of her phone and sent a lie into cyberspace.

ROSE: Not tonight. Sick. Sorry.

She almost sat her phone back onto the bedside table but kept it in hand. No way that was the end of the conversation.

MARIA: Girl, you ain't sick. Get your ass out here!

Oh, good. She was belligerent drunk.

ROSE: Seriously. Head's killing me. Another night.

MARIA: You ain't fooling me. You turn your phone off when you're sick.

This was the problem with lifelong best friends. They knew every damn thing about you.

ROSE: Look just not feeling it tonight. I'll come out next weekend.

MARIA: That's what you said last weekend.

It was hard to argue with that. Rose had been dodging and cancelling plans with Maria for months now.

MARIA: Come on. You gotta come. The whole department made it out. Even Luke is here!

That was low. Maria knew about her crush on Luke. When she warned Rose about the company policy she added a slap to the face. Let her know the man was out of her league. "You ain't his type, hermana."

Those five words were like gas on her burning insecurities. Maria had always been that classic Latin beauty all the boys liked. With the perfect face and the perfect body.

Rose wasn't ugly. But standing next to Maria for twenty years…well, it was a challenge. Rose was a bit too tall, her face a bit too round, and her curves a bit too thick. She looked like a fertility goddess. She'd made peace with her looks. And had lost a lot of weight over the years. But when Maria said that six months ago, *You ain't his type, hermana*, she was fourteen again listening to Nick Ramsey stumble to find a nice way to tell her she was too fat to date.

But this time, she got the hot guy. She had him right here. And Maria was trying to use him to get her to come out. She really could be a manipulative bitch sometimes. It would serve her right if Rose did come down there.

That's when it hit her. She could end this conversation here and now. Her thumbs got to work.

ROSE: Luke the home body? Bullshit! Pics or it didn't happen!

This time she did sit her phone down. Maria couldn't produce Luke. So, she would ignore her message until tomorrow and make something up. Someone called for shots or she forgot to respond after the DJ played her favorite song. But the one thing she wouldn't do was reply tonight.

Except she did.

This oughta be good.

Rose opened Maria's message and forgot how to breathe. How to read. How to talk. How to think. She snapped her head to the left to see her guest still snoozing beside her. Then back to the picture.

It was impossible. Just fucking impossible. But it was right there on the screen in front of her. Luke. Her Luke. Luke who was asleep beside her. At Phantoms. With Maria. This wasn't an old picture. Maria was wearing the dress she'd bought a few days ago.

Rose swallowed a lump of panic. *Calm down. There's lots of possible explanations.*

ROSE: He does look kinda like him. That his brother or something?

MARIA: What're you talkin about? It's Luke.

But it couldn't be.

ROSE: That's not him and you know it. Come clean.

MARIA: Luke doesn't have any brothers. You been crushin on this man six months and never talked to him?

She had a point. At the office, Rose and Luke mostly threw banter back and forth. Bickered their way through the day. Compared sales figures. But they'd never really talked until this whole thing started up, and even that wasn't exactly filled with conversation. The truth is she didn't really know him.

How *had* this started? The whole thing had been a whirlwind. She remembered running into him at the bodega down the street. He helped her carry groceries back to her apartment. And then…

Suddenly, she felt ill. Panic was working its way back up. The soreness of her muscles and the smoldering pleasure in her loins felt like a violation.

Rose dashed out of bed and hurried into her living room. She couldn't stay there next to him. She curled up on her couch, her body and breath trembling. God, she wanted to scream. Call for help. Tell Maria to come rescue her. But part of her still struggled to find a reasonable explanation.

Okay, girl. Relax. Think. One of these guys is Luke. The other isn't. You just gotta figure out which is which.

But how? Three months of hurried dinners and bedroom fun hadn't exactly equipped her to separate fact from fiction. But she had to start somewhere.

ROSE: Did he come alone?

MARIA: He showed up with Steve.

Steve! He left Solace Med a month ago. But she still had his number. Maybe he could give her something.

ROSE: Are you and Luke really at Phantom's?

STEVE: Yep!

She took a deep breath and started typing. And then erasing. Then typing again. Then erasing.

She started a half dozen sentences but didn't know how to finish any of them.

Then came another message.

STEVE: Not chatting with you on here. You wanna talk to me you gotta come out.

Nothing felt real anymore. Everything was wrong, but she couldn't figure out how. Maybe it was time to tell Maria everything.

Just then, a message came in.

MARIA: Don't pester Steve. He really needs tonight to go well.

That didn't make any sense.

ROSE: Why's that?

MARIA: You didn't hear this from me. But Steve and Luke are on a date tonight.

That clicked hard.

ROSE: A date? You sure?

MARIA: Yeah. I know you had a thing for him but I told you. You ain't his type. Just don't spread it around ok? Luke's not really out yet.

So, that was it. Luke was gay. And the man in her bed very much wasn't. That meant…what *did* that mean? That bedroom Luke was a fake? That Phantom's Luke was a fake? She couldn't really tell.

Rose was startled by the sudden silence of her bedroom TV. And terrified by the footsteps heading her way. When Luke emerged from the bedroom, she almost screamed. He shambled his way into the living room rubbing his sleepy eyes. "You coming back to bed?" he asked.

"Um. Yeah. In a minute."

He nodded an okay and stumbled into her bathroom.

The world started to spin in a cyclone of panic.

What should she do? Should she leave?

Of course, *you should!* She yelled inwardly. *That other Luke might not be real but at least you wouldn't be alone with him!*

She would leave. Rush out the door as soon as he fell back to sleep.

The toilet flushed. The sink ran. The bathroom door opened and produced a Luke. "What're you up to?"

"Oh. I'm just…" her words were cut short as he started toward her.

It took everything she had not to jump off the couch when he sat down beside her. "Who texted you at this hour?"

"Maria," she answered quickly. "She's out at Phantom's. Been trying to get me to come out. You know how she is."

He glanced at her phone and then her face.

Something in him changed in that moment. The lamplight reflected something in his eyes. Not anger. Not jealousy. But something unsettling. Something twisted.

Malice. That was the word. And a gleeful malice at that. He had the smile of a mischievous boy about to pluck the wings off a fly or rip the head off his sister's favorite doll. And the words that came from his grinning mouth were enough to stab her in the chest.

"Is Luke there?"

Kareem Miskel was born in Chicago and raised in a small Illinois town called Mattoon where he graduated high school. He loves to write fantasy, science-fiction, and horror of all kinds. He tends to prefer constructing smaller narratives, tending toward flash fiction, short stories, or novellas. Today he lives in Bartlett, Illinois and works in customer service.

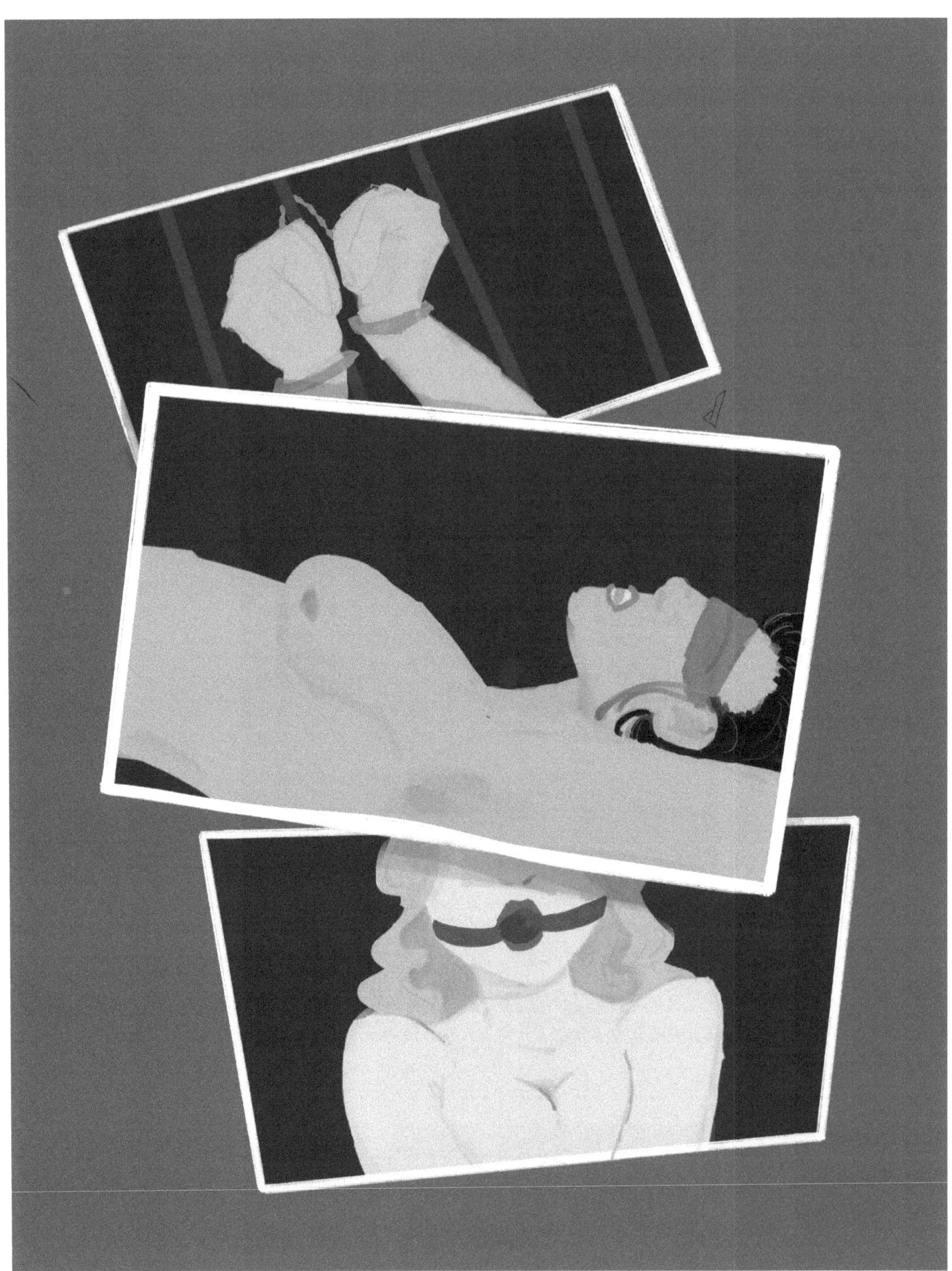

Art by Vesqid

Contractual

By

P.L. McMillan

USE OF VOICE, IMAGE, AND LIKENESS. Contracted Subject gives the Company permission to use any and all of their voice, image, and likeness for the purposes of advertising and promoting the Product and/or the Company, and/or for other purposes deemed appropriate by the Company in its reasonable discretion.

"You'll be great," Lily says. "Just keep smiling!"

Speaker identified. Previous contact: Lily Boone. 95% assessment certainty. More information?

I shake my head slightly, the prompt fades. Applause erupts.

"That's your cue, babe!" Lily says and pushes me forward.

Possible obstruction identified: curtain — 86% assessment certainty. More information?

I feel the fabric against my face, my body, then release into heat. There's rising applause that deafens. I smile. As instructed.

USE OF PERSONAL INFORMATION. Any information and data collected by the Product during the experimental trial will be sent to the Company at the end of every business day. The Contracted Subject acknowledges and agrees to allow the Company to use recorded data to further develop the performance of the Product.

"It'll be booting up now. Any pain?" the nurse asks.

I shake my head, despite the dull throb echoing through my brain.

"Dizziness?"

My head feels strange, alien, stuffed to overflowing.

"Mrs. Alasdair?"

"I — " My head vibrates, my brain fills with static.

Identified user: Nettie Lynn
Alasdair. Confirm?

"I — there's thoughts in my head, appearing — " I press my hands against my temples, my brain running hot, stifling.

"Excellent, are you receiving a confirmation request?"

The strange feeling of a message pulses again: Identified user: Nettie Lynn Alasdair. Confirm?

Not words or images, just thoughts. A stranger's thoughts in my mind.

"What is this? What's happening?"

"I need you to say or think 'confirm'. Do you understand?"

Confirm. "Confirm." I say and think at the same time.

Authorized user accepted. Welcome Nettie! I am your new InSightFull v0.0.

"I wasn't expecting…"

"Are you experiencing some discomfort?"

Speaker: mid-forties femme-presenting humanoid. Black hair, brown skin, brown eyes. 90% certainty in assessment. More information?

"I wasn't expecting it to feel like… thoughts," I say. "Do you have black hair?"

The nurse laughs. "Glad to hear it's working. InSightFull responds to both mental and verbal commands. Don't forget your first physical is in thirty days."

PAYMENT TERMS AND CONDITIONS.

Contracted Subject agrees to participate in Company's experimental trial in exchange for ownership of Product upon completion and one lump sum of $100,000 USD. Should Contracted Subject resign from the trial period, they will relinquish Product within seven business days and uphold the terms of Appendix 1A: Non-Disclosure Addendum.

"Does Carl know?" Mary asks.

New object in range. Mug containing dark liquid, steam indicates high temperature. Caution is advised. 70% certainty in assessment.

I reach out. InSightFull predicts my intent. I feel a kind of pulse in my head, its frequency increasing as I move my hand outward. The pulses increase into a steady hum and I find the mug easily, feel a flare of satisfaction despite the pounding behind my eyes.

"No, he thinks I am just visiting you," I say, finding the cream.

"He's so controlling," Mary adds.

"I don't know if I would say it was controlling…"

"He tried to forbid you from getting a free implant that could help you be independent of him," Mary says. "I did warn you before you got married, Nettie."

"He was worried about the side effects, Mary. InSightFull isn't FDA approved. It's still in testing."

"I'm just saying, I've never trusted him."

I try to imagine how the conversation would go, telling Carl I'd lied, that I'd gone behind his back and gotten the surgery. He worried. I couldn't blame him. The bills, my struggle to find regular work, his increasing workload. I just wished he would rely on me more, talk to me more, instead of just getting frustrated.

"You're so far away from everything in that stupid fucking cabin."

"He just wants to keep me safe, Mary. The city isn't really safe," I echo Carl's words.

"He wants to keep you isolated. Common red flag for abusive relationships," Mary replies. "It happens all the time in my true crime podcasts."

"Mary, please." The pounding intensifies, like clamps pinching each optic nerve. "Can I have an aspirin or something?"

"Stay with me, Nettie. Just for a month or so, okay?" Mary's voice moves away, returns. "I can talk to my boss, I'm sure we could find a job for you. Data entry or something."

InSightFull identifies the pill bottle as containing sedatives. I pour a couple pills into my palm, allowing it to use my optic nerves to read the imprinted lettering and correct itself to generic aspirin. Satisfied, I swallow both dry.

"I appreciate the offer," I reply.

"Are you still thinking of leaving him?" Mary says.

I forced out all the air in my lungs in a heavy sigh. "I don't know, Mary. I… I guess I want to see if he'll go back to being the Carl I fell in love with."

"What? Cause you can see now?"

"I can't see — never mind." I press my palms against my temples. "The money I'm getting will help with bills and stuff. Maybe with less money stress, things will get better."

"He's showing you who he really is, Nettie. How long are you going to pretend it can get better?"

"Marriages go through rough patches, it's normal."

"How come he never lets anyone over then?"

"He just gets anxious, having guests in his living space — "

"When are you going to stop making excuses for him. Nettie?"

POSSIBLE HEALTH RISKS. Potential side effects associated with the Product include, but are not limited to: nausea, vomiting, confusion, glitches/errors, headaches, nose bleeds, misidentification of objects/persons, inner ear canal pain, general fatigue. Severity and occurrence of these side effects may vary. Any experienced side effects should be promptly reported to the Company contact provided.

Carl is home when I return. I can hear him in the kitchen, the air is humid, smelling of tomato and onion.

Footsteps approach, ones I recognize. I set my bag down.

"Babe! You're home!"

Speaker identified: masc-presenting humanoid, short cropped red hair, blue eyes. Late thirties. 95% certainty in assessment. "How's that sister of yours?"

InSightFull alerts me so I don't flinch as he pulls me in for a hug, picking up his name from my thoughts — Carl Alasdair.

"She's good. The baby is doing well."

"She still talking shit about me?" He laughs but there's bitterness in his voice.

"Carl…" I follow him into the kitchen.

I direct my face towards the stove.

`Stainless steel pots. Left pot containing boiling liquid. Water. 61% certainty in assessment. Right pot contains mixture of red sauce, tomatoes, mushrooms, onion, ground meat.74% certainty is assessment.`

I sniff. The acidity of the tomatoes overwhelms everything else.

"Are there mushrooms in this?" I ask.

Carl barks out a harsh laugh. "Why would I put mushrooms in it? We've been together for eight years now, I know they make you shit yourself."

I grimace at his choice of words.

"You okay?" He's close. I can feel his body heat, smell his sweat.

"I'm fine," I lie, hoping he can't see the small incision mark behind my right ear, one that Mary promised me wasn't noticeable.

INFORMATION STORAGE AND USE. Contracted Subject understands that the Product will be recording all visual data for use in advancing and developing the Product's analytical and identification programs. Contracted Subject consents to the collection and use of such information. All collected data used in training and advancing Product is owned by the Company. The Company may use this data for any purpose deemed necessary, including commercial.

The toilet's flush is thunderous. It's late. The house is swallowed by the hush only deep night has. I don't need InSightFull's guidance to find the sink, the hand soap, the towel. It's all memorized routine now.

My lower belly cramps.

Was it the dinner Carl made me? I think of InSightFull identifying mushrooms in the sauce. I remember Carl's harsh laugh.

Another cramp ripples through my guts and I press my fists to where it aches. It could be a reaction to the pain medication I'd been given.

I wait until the last cramp passes, my belly roiling uneasily, then I softly return to the bedroom. Despite the darkness, InSightFull notifies me of the dresser, the foot of the bed, the closet door. I locate the edge of the covers.

`Object identified: photograph in plain black frame. Located above nightstand on left hand side of bed. Black and white photo of naked femme-presenting humanoid, lying on black sheets, handcuffed. 83% certainty in assessment.`

The pictures above our nightstands are from our wedding. Carl had them printed and framed himself. Pictures of our kiss at the alter, our first dance.

Tiptoeing around the bed, I stop in front of his nightstand, reach out, touch the frame — guided by InSightFull's nudges. I prompt it to analyze the image again.

`Object rescanned: photograph in plain black frame. Photo of`

nude femme-presenting humanoid,
handcuffed. Short dark hair. Mid-
twenties. 90% certainty in
assessment.

Stumbling, numb, I go to the dresser, avoiding the floorboards that creak as best I can. There are five more wedding photos above it. Or at least, that's what Carl had told me.

Five photos, black and white, nude women. Two tied, three gagged, two blindfolded. InSightFull is 85% certain.

I shake my head, pressing the back of my hand to my mouth. It's dark. The AI could be struggling to identify the subject of the photographs. It has to be struggling.

Another cramp grips me.

"Babe?"

I jump at the sound of his voice, sleepy and hoarse behind me.

"Just an upset stomach," I say and return to the bathroom.

CARE OBLIGATION. Contracted Subject is responsible for reporting any and all issues regarding Product use within 3 hours. Any delay, damages, or bodily harm as a result of unreported Product issues will solely fall on Contracted Subject.

"I — I understand InSightFull is in a trial period but — " I'm sitting in the bathtub, the curtain drawn, sink tap running, door locked. Anything to act as a sound barrier between me and Carl.

"I just — I need to know, how can I verify — "

I press the knuckles of my free hand into my forehead, digging and kneading.

"No, I don't want to halt the trial — "

There's a trio of loud knocks on the door, I can practically feel it rattling in its frame. "Babe, you done in there?"

"Just a moment!" I call, free hand cupped over the phone's receiver.

The doorknob jiggles brightly. "You stuck in the toilet or something?"

I used to find his humour more… endearing.

"Just a fucking minute!" I snap as he knocks again and again. "No, not you, sorry — no, it's not an emergency. I — "

My chest tightens slowly, the sounds grow, overwhelm me, suffocates. My head throbs. The hissing of the sink, the woman in my ear, Carl at the door, his fists on the wood.

"I just need to know how can I verify it's working? How can I know? Don't you get the visual recordings sent to you or something?"

"Babe? Seriously, are you okay?"

"I'm not saying it's not working! I just need to — "

Over it all, all the sounds, I hear the assertive bright click of a lock opening. I end the call, jamming my phone into the pocket of my jeans. The bathroom door squeaks and I desperately scramble to come up with an excuse, while also wrestling with my disbelief that Carl has just come barging in.

"Jesus, Nettie! Why didn't you answer me?"

My tongue trips over anger at my privacy being violated and guilt at hiding something from him. "Can't I get some — "

"Oh my God, babe! You're bleeding!"

His hands are on me, pulling me to sit on the edge of the tub. He cups my face, turning my head up.

"Blood?" I ask, raising a hand to cover the surgical site.

"Your nose, fuck's sake, you're soaked! Just fucking drenched in it."

His body heat fades, I hear activity at the sink.

`Identified contact: Carl Alistair. Activity: washing dishes. 86% certainty in assessment.`

I shake my head.

`Reassessing.`

I feel him approach and kneel in front of me, smell steam, then a hot cloth presses against my face. He had been wetting a cloth.

`Activity: wetting a cloth. Data noted.`

"Shit, maybe we should take you to the ER. Is this a normal amount of blood?"

Panic blooms, not for the blood, but for what would show if we went to the ER and I was examined. I push Carl away, taking the cloth from him. I can smell the wet hot copper now. "I'm fine, it's nothing."

"Babe, I know you can't tell, but this is a lot of fucking blood." His hands are on me again, pulling me up, gripping, tugging.

"Carl!"

He pulls me through the bathroom door, my elbow bouncing off the threshold in a way I know will bruise. I slip on the floor in my socks, slamming to my knees, pain lancing through my body. His hands are all over me, so much so that InSightFull identifies him as three people before it corrects itself.

"Stop, Carl!" I swing out with the now cooling wet cloth and feel an impact, hear a sodden smack.

The hands shrink away, accompanied with a sharp intake of breath.

"Now there's blood all over my fucking shirt, Nettie," he says. "Disgusting. Jesus Christ."

"I don't need the ER, I'm fine! Why won't you just listen to me?"

"Fuck sakes. All you had to do was say so, not ruin my favourite fucking white polo!"

`Reassessing. White shirt. Correcting data.`

He walks away, I feel his footsteps reverberating through the floor, up into my knees. I urge InSightFull to audit its data.

It had identified Carl as wearing a black t-shirt.

CONFIDENTIAL INFORMATION. Contracted Subject acknowledges and agrees to keep confidential and not reveal to any person, press, company their participation in Product experimental trial. Only persons approved by Company in advance may be informed of Contracted Subject's participation and Product information, usage, and intent. Any breach of this clause must be made immediately aware to the Company.

Carl is sulking in his workshop, out behind the garage. I am alone in the kitchen, phone in hand, wondering if I should call Mary. She'll overreact. Or maybe I'm underreacting.

Maybe she'll tell me to leave the experiment, get the implant removed. My nose itches from the thick crusts of dried blood that rim it. I set my phone down instead. I need the money. I need the freedom. I was briefed to expect side effects, that InSightFull would be learning day by day. I just had to give it time, do what I was told to help speed the training.

Step one. Map each room.

Slowly, I make my way through the kitchen and living room, marking the perimeter of each, trying to pause in front of each piece of furniture, each window, each door. InSightFull marks each one, asking for confirmation, which I do by touching the items myself.

I make some coffee, InSightFull guiding me so I fumble less, find things faster.

Next: front hall, front door, out to the front porch, I can feel the sunlight on my face, smell the evergreens that ring the house.

InSightFull guides me around a fallen branch as I go behind the garage and to Carl's studio. His passion is woodworking, creating sculptures and ornate furniture that people rarely buy. InSightFull alerts me as I approach one sculpture, then a statue, another sculpture. Each one apparently too ill-defined for InSightFull to identify what they were supposed to resemble. I feel the sculptures briefly with my free hand and am just as confused at their planes and angles as InSightFull.

At the shed door, I listen. Beyond is a soft whir of a saw. It sounds off to me. Woodworking is a harsh hobby — splintery crescendos, barking breaks, whining saws. But the saw sounds as though its eating through something soft, wet.

I shiver, push open the door.

Immediately the sound stops.

"Nettie? What are you doing here?" Carl snaps, footsteps thudding across the floor.

InSightFull lets me know he's coming towards me, then lists off the tools that surround me. I stop in front of a table it identified and hold out the coffee.

"Thought you could use some fuel!" I say.

`Contents on table closest to user Nettie: 2 by 1 foot plank of wood. Human arm. Hand saw. Two screwdrivers. Box of nails. More information?`

"I — " I freeze, trying to play back what InSightFull had reeled off.

"You know I don't like you in here." Carl takes the coffee mug from me. InSightFull notes that he places it on the table, next to the hand saw. "It's dangerous. There are tools everywhere, you could hurt yourself!"

"Tell me what you're up to, let's spend time together!" I feel guilty for keeping secrets. We've never kept secrets from each other. Or, at least, I know I've never kept secrets from him…until now. I slide past him. "Is it a new sculpture?"

"Babe, let's talk outside. You're gonna knock something over."

But I don't. InSightFull makes sure of it. I slip around a chair on the right, a chest of tools on the left. It gives me pleasure to walk freely, not to fumble or reach.

`Passing 2 foot tall mask. Crude features. 32% certainty in assessment.` "Did you get a custom order?"

"Nothing like that, babe. Come on, there's just saws and shit back there." His hand brushes over my back and I slip away so he can't grab my elbow like he always does.

On the right: tree trunk. 87% certainty in assessment.

I reach out with my fingers and feel the rough bark, the faintest raised rings marking the years the tree lived.

On the left: humanoid leg on floor. 63% certainty in assessment.

I stumble.

"See, babe? I told you!"

I kneel, reaching out, InSightFull pings me, and I have to know. I have to feel it. I swear I smell copper, old and musty. It makes my throat itch.

His arm finds my elbow and he pulls me to my feet.

RELEASE OF LIABILITY. Contracted Subject understands that there are risks associated with their use of Product, such as physical and/or psychological injury, pain, suffering, illness, disfigurement, temporary or permanent disability, death or economic loss. Contracted Subject assumes all risks of their participation in Product test trials, whether known or unknown to them, including any events incidental to the use of the Product.

"You found a fucking arm? Like a dead human arm?" Mary hisses.

"I don't know what it was, I didn't get to check."

"I'm coming to get you, okay? Holy shit. Charles? Charles! I gotta get my sister — "

"Mary! Just chill, okay?"

"Chill? Chill!? My sister finds a decapitated arm in her husband's workshop and tells me to chill?"

"I — for one thing, you don't decapitate an arm, secondly — "

"Charles! I need you to watch baby Chuck for a few — "

"Secondly, I don't even know it was an arm. InSightFull is still learning! I just need to go back in and check. I need to feel it for myself."

"Oh fuck no, Nettie. You wanna be the stupid slut who ends up being in one of my true crime podcasts who should've known better?"

"What crime? There's no crime, okay?" I try and sound calm but my heart is racing.

"I am coming to get you. End of story."

"Come on, it's late. If you're really worried, come by tomorrow, okay?"

She sighs, the baby cries. "Fine. First thing in the morning. Don't you fucking dare go back to that shed."

I wait until I hear Carl's soft snores before sneaking out of the bedroom, barefoot across the hardwood floors. InSightFull guides me out into the night and back to the shed. My nerves are locked tight as my entire body thrums with anxiety.

I tug on the door handle and the door is locked. I can't go back. I have to know. I circle around the shed.

Object identified: window. 98% certainty in assessment.

I reach out and find glass, probe until my fingertips locate the bottom of the window and I push up. With a soft squeak, the pane rises. A part of me thrills, lightning in my veins, I never would have done this without InSightFull. Never would have risked it.

It guides me as I crawl through the window. My elation soon withers as I tiptoe through the workshop. InSightFull identifies the mask, the stump, the wooden planks. It calls out the tools, the half-finished chair. But the leg is gone.

If it'd ever been there at all.

I shake my head. As amazing as InSightFull is, it's still new, still learning. "I'm an idiot."

My knees ache from crawling through the window and I am pretty sure my palms are likely scraped up from the heat and stinging, so I decide to exit out the door.

InSightFull pings me in the right direction. I slip as my left foot skids in a cold tacky puddle on the floor. I stumble, my feet squelch on the floor.

I tilt my head down.

`Object identified: stain. Origin and composition unknown.`

It wasn't like Carl to leave a mess.

Kneeling, I let InSightFull have a closer view.

`Reassess: liquid, unknown composition.`

Dipping two fingers into the sludge, I bring them to my nose and sniff. Metallic, sour smelling.

It reminds me of my nosebleed.

My heart tolls in my chest. I find door, then the light switch that will illuminate the shed and give InSightFull a better chance at identifying whatever is on the floor.

I don't sense the light come on but I hear the click and kneel again.

`Reassess: puddle, semi-dry liquid, burgundy in colour with black, cracking perimeter.`

I choke down a cry, rocking back on bare heels that are sticky with whatever is pooled out in front of me.

Blood?

`User suggested input: blood. Reassessing. Possibility of blood — 78%.`

The door squeaks and I scream, standing, whirling.

"Nettie? What the hell are you doing in here?" Carl snaps. "How did you get in here?"

"Carl, what is that?" I point where I remember the stain being. Oh fuck, this is exactly what Mary would tell me not to do. Do not confront the killer all alone.

"What are you talking about, Nettie?" he says, dangerously calm. "There's nothing there."

"The pool of — of whatever that shit is," I say. "Whatever is all over my feet, Carl."

"That's just wine, Nettie. I spilled it earlier."

"Don't lie to me, okay? Don't you fucking lie to me. You don't drink. *We* don't drink." InSightFull alerts me as he approaches and I stumble back.

"I — I'm sorry, babe. I *have* been drinking," he says. "I had a couple of drinks with the guys after work last month, and then I just couldn't stop. With the stress and everything…"

"That's not wine," I hiss, my nose coated in the stench of copper. "What about the pictures in the bedroom?"

"The what?" InSightFull alerts me as he lunges, reaching for me.

I dodge, tumbling into a table rattling with tools. I grab one — a hammer, swing it in front of me. "Stay back, Carl."

"What the fuck is wrong with you, Nettie?" he snarls.

"The pictures in the bedroom." I point the hammer at him. "They aren't of us or our wedding, are they?"

"What are you talking about, of course they're of us!"

"Yeah and that's just wine on the floor."

He's trying to sneak around the workbench. I turn to face him, hammer still raised.

"You don't know what you're talking about, Nettie." He pauses in front of me. "I'm sorry I lied to you about being sober, okay? Just calm the fuck down."

"Let's call the cops then," I say. "Let them come and tell me what that really is."

"Jesus Christ, Nettie. Are *you* drunk?" He steps closer.

"Stay back, Carl. Stay the fuck back or I *will* use this."

He lunges.

REPRESENTATION. In the event or need of legal and/or public representation, Contracted Subject waives their right to choose their own representative while using Product. All legal and marketing representation will be provided by the Company. Contracted Subject will obey all decisions as made by the Company legal/marketing representative. Failure to do so will result in repossession of Product and $100,000,000 USD fine.

"Mrs. Alistair declines to answer any questions at this time." My Company appointed lawyer, Minh Nguyen, distracts the reporters outside the courthouse, allowing InSightFull to guide me straight into the hired car that's waiting for us.

The AC blasts me, freezing my sweat to my skin. The car rocks as Mihn joins me.

"Couldn't have gone any better," Mihn says.

I can still hear the echoes of Carl's mother crying in the courtroom.

The defense lawyer describing the destruction to Carl's cranium, the brains on the hammer head, the sloughing of his face, the blood that pooled with the wine on the floor.

Mihn's damnation of Carl of a drunken husband.

Mary crying on the stand, painting Carl as a man who left bruises and controlled his blind wife.

I feel the phantom hot splatter of blood across my face, the thicker impacts of what may have been brains. I want to vomit. I want to forget.

A hand falls on my knee and I start, turning to another passenger I had no idea was there.

"Congratulations on the settlement, Nettie," a woman says. "Of course, there is the matter of paying back the fees for representation. I'm Lily Boone, Vulpes Company PR representative. I'll walk you through what you'll be doing for us from now on."

P.L. McMillan's short fiction has appeared in a variety of anthologies and magazines such as Cosmic Horror Monthly, Strange Lands Short Stories, Negative Space, and AHH! That's What I Call Horror, as well as adapted to audio forms for podcasts like NoSleep and Nocturnal Transmissions. In addition to her short stories, McMillan's debut collection, What Remains When The Stars Burn Out, and debut novella, Sisters of the Crimson Vine, are available now. Besides being a fiction writer, PLM has experience as an editor (Howls from the Dark Ages and The Darkness Beyond The Stars: An Anthology of Space Horror), hosts PLM Talks on Youtube (interviewing peers and professionals in the horror industry), and is the co-host of a horror writing craft podcast, Dead Languages Podcast. Find her at plmcmillan.com

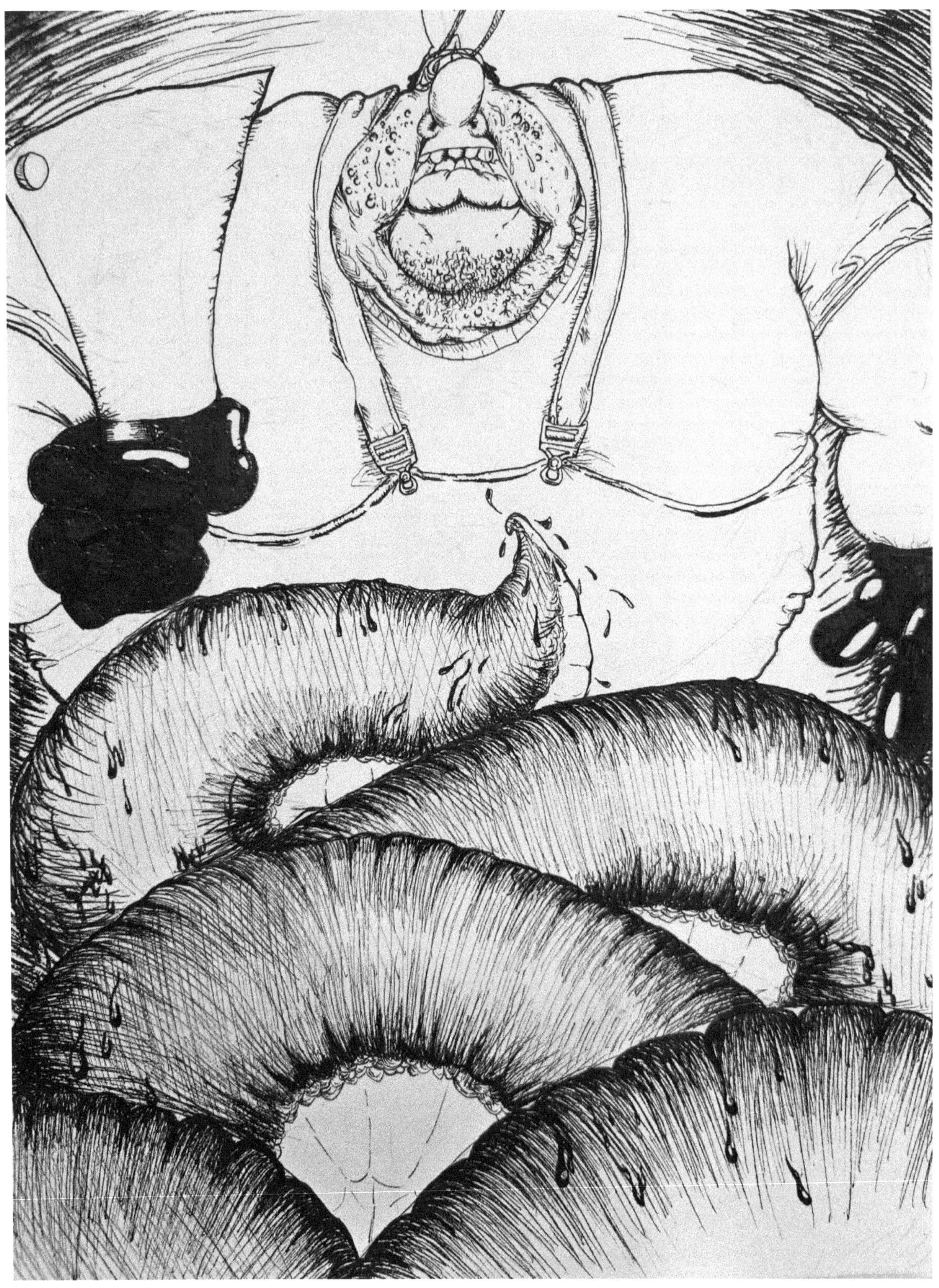

Art by Mike David

Happy Hour at Harry's Hole in the Wall

By

Joshua Dobson

The men hunched over the bar are workers from the nearby factory. They're missing more pieces than a garage sale jigsaw puzzle. The goggles the amputees wear while trying not to lose any more body parts to the machines protect their eyes from the soot which encrusts the entirety of their faces save for domino masks of skin, white as the bellies of vampirized cavefish, around their dull dead doll eyes. They sit silently, only moving to pick up their glasses and raise them to their mouths before returning them to the bar for further visual contemplation. None of them so much as glance up when the door of the dive whose sign proclaims it: *Harry's Hole in the Wall* creaks open on rusty squeaking hinges.

Against the rear wall sits a small stage with a crooked brass pole rising from its center.

The naked woman dancing atop the stage is skinny as a starving snake. The skin shrink-wrapped around her protruding skeleton is caked with grey dust. Slug trails of clean white skin extend from her haunted eyes down her sunken cheeks; the tears which carved these tracks drip from her chin.

An old fashioned hand cranked turntable sits on a rickety table at the side of the stage and belches out the kinda music they used to play on the Ed Sullivan show while some dude in a tuxedo balanced spinning dinner plates atop pool cues. The record pops and hisses as the crying stripper bucks and grinds her hips before segueing into shaking her shoulders to make the rubbery pink tassels on her pasties spin.

The mirror behind the stage faces the mirror behind the bar and creates an infinity of weeping, dancing girls each tinier than the last.

"Please help me," the stripper moans piteously at Butch as he stalks towards the bar.

"Please mister, I'm in hell. This is hell, please help me," the stripper begs; her entreaty is cut short when the record she's dancing to skips and she seems to skip right along with it, beginning her routine again with the bucking, grinding hips giving way to twirling tassels. Then the record skips and she repeats the routine all over again.

Butch stops to watch her go through her loop a couple times before ignoring her,as do the redneck behind the bar and the soot encrusted workers.

Butch saunters up to the bar.

"Look here buddy I don't want no trouble, I'm all paid up with Mr. W. and the fuzz," the redneck bartender says, one hand gripping something under the bar.

Butch briefly considers taking whatever the redneck has hidden under the bar and sticking it up the fucker's ass. But he doesn't, instead he says,

"Teddy's dead."

"Shitfire," the redneck says.

"I'm his replacement," Butch says.

"You get two free shots, one before, one after," the redneck drawls, "Mid-shelf only. What's your poison?"

Butch downs the shot of rotgut and checks his watch.

"Please, please kill me," the record skip stripper pleads while Butch rises from the wobbly stool.

"Good luck," the redneck says as Butch marches towards the door to the bathroom.

The door to the shitter has a sheet of paper nailed to it by four big ass Martin Luther nailing shit to a door type nails; "Out of Order!!!"scrawled on the paper in red marker.

The lock on the bathroom door is both the newest and most expensive object in the shithole dive. Butch removes the fob from his pocket and sorts through the keys until he finds the right one.

After stepping into the lavatory, he closes and locks the door behind him.

He sets his attaché case on the counter, unlocks, and opens it. Then he takes off his jacket and hangs it from the hook on the door. The yellow rubber apron he dons is the type worn by slaughterhouse workers. The safety goggles are probably not too dissimilar to those worn by the partially devoured factory workers while they breathe in soot for twelve hours a day. The thick black rubber gloves are at once both fetishistic and industrial.

Butch spreads a crisp clean towel over the counter and begins to carefully lay out his gear.

As his fingers curl around the handle of the meat cleaver, Butch feels an intense desire to bury the blade in his flesh. He stares at the silver mirror of the cleaver's blade, but instead of his own reflection staring back at him he sees a screaming woman with no limbs howling in either agony or ecstasy as blood slow motion gushes from her freshly amputated stumps.

He sets the cleaver on the counter and continues laying out his other tools in a precise orderly row.

He checks his watch.

"Bet ya couldn't cut your own head off with a single swing," a mocking voice hisses inside his skull as he picks up the cleaver. He desperately wants to prove the snake voice wrong. But he ignores it and imagines a brick wall which holds back the voices and the strange urges they inspire (a trick he learned from a movie).

"What happens to you is gonna make what happened to Teddy seem like a walk in the park ya piece a shit," a growling death metal voice rumbles from beneath the bottom of his brain as he checks his watch again.

There are three stalls; the glory hole is in the partition between the center stall and the one furthest from the door.

There's a stain on the filthy yellow tiled floor beneath the glory hole. A Rorschach blot tumor colored a bruise-like purple which seems to pulse and squiggle as he stares at it.

A string of occult symbols are graffitto'd around the glory hole through which peers an incredibly realistic painting of an unblinking bloodshot eye which is inscribed on the wall of the next stall. There's a sign on the wall above the glory hole which reads: *Employees Must Wear Eye Protection Near Glory Hole!* Beneath the hole in the partition a graffito scrawled in a spidery hand: "4 a goo slime call 666-6969".

Butch checks his watch then sits down on the toilet and waits, cleaver gripped in his hand, eyes trained on the glory hole.

Time moves strangely in the bathroom, or maybe his watch is broken cuz when he checks it again it says it's five minutes before the last time he checked it.

Every ounce of mental fiber he possesses is dedicated to resisting the nearly overwhelming urge to whip his tackle out and jam it into the glory hole, from which faintly whispering, nearly inaudible voices seem to drift.

He imagines the brick wall as he resists an intense urge to put his ear up to hole so that he might hear what the seductive yet menacing whispers are hissing. Even without knowing what they're saying he gets the gist of it from the tone, the whispers are both an enticement and a threat, inviting him to partake of his own doom (and giving him permission to enjoy it).

The chorus of whispering voices suddenly grows louder and a gush of hot humid air that stinks like rotten goat meat and mushrooms boiling in blood and diseased vaginal secretions heated by burning brimstone oozes from the glory hole.

There's a sizzling electric chair noise from the ceiling, then the fluorescent lights go dark.

The darkness is filled with the sound of all the toilets flushing simultaneously; beneath the rush of water and the hungrily sucking vacuum noise is a sound like the gurgling screams of a drowning man.

Then light, unlike any earthly color spills from the portal, like some pestilent luminescence oozing from a diseased star covered with bruises and infected sores. It isn't merely some combination of colors never previously combined; it's an entirely new color, some wavelength of light his eyes have never absorbed before. The rancid phosphorescence doesn't behave like light; it isn't projected like a beam or ray, rather it blooms in the air like a swirling cloud of smoke or vapor.

A slimy, glistening black-purple tentacle unfurls from the glory hole, wriggling like a beckoning finger curling in a come-hither gesture. The tentacle doesn't have suction cups. It's a smooth, horse-wiener-length whip of flesh, soda-can-thick where it emerges from/disappears into the glory hole portal but tapering to a pointy dunce cap shaped tip.

The writhing of the tentacle is like bad claymation, a film with missing frames or laggy video. The wrongly wriggling thing seems more like a pseudopod extruded from the body of an amoeba rather than the solid fleshy tentacle of some squid-o-pus type mollusk; it seems more a viscous goo than something solid.

The safety goggles are fogging up with condensed moisture and Butch feels a nearly overwhelming urge to remove them. Brick wall, he thinks.

He glances through the open door of the stall at the mirror behind the sink on the far wall. Nothing visible in the stall on the 'pitching' side of the glory hole. His face reflected in the mirror is horribly distorted, trembling all seizure-y, blurry, mouth open wide in a silent scream.

Black snakes of twisting smoke rise from the tentacle to swirl and spiral in the fetid air. The shiny black slime which drips from the pseudopod beckons Butch to lick it off the floor, begging him to kneel before the glory hole and take the tentacle in his mouth.

Resist the call of the tentacle. Brick wall.

His mind is flooded with an extremely detailed vision of the squirming tentacle plunging through his eyeball—which pops in a seething gush of KY-Jelly-like vitreous humor—and burrowing into the wrinkled meat of his brain. Some part of him desperately wants nothing more than the tentacle buried in his skull.

Resist. Brick wall.

Butch raises the cleaver white-knuckle gripped in his gloved hand and brings the blade chopping down into the frenetically squiggling tendril.

The tentacle must be tougher than its soft-slimy appearance suggests, the blade only bites halfway through the shaft and an explosion of steaming hot, black-purple goo sprays from the stump which rapidly retracts half its length back into the glory hole portal.

Hard to pull the blade out, pressure inside the tentacles suck-grips it. Butch's hand is shaking like a hanged man's legs. He yanks hard as he can, nearly falls on his ass, recovers, aims for the same spot, brings the blade down again, misses the site of the previous chop, but manages to sink the cleaver three quarters of the way through the tentacle.

His third blow hacks the tentacle in twain. It falls to the floor seemingly in slow motion.

The blighted light mushroom-clouding from the glory hole portal grows dimmer and dimmer until it dissolves completely. Likewise the frenzied babble of the whispering voices grows quieter and quieter until it lurks just a nun's cunt hair above the level of inaudibility.

Butch just sits there in the utter darkness for a moment or two breathing heavy like an asthmatic obscene phone caller, then there's a Taser sizzle and the fluorescent lights pop back on.

He stares at the severed tentacle writhing on the floor like a slug recoiling from a shower of salt. Can't help but feel like it's trying to tell him something, as if its writhing is a form of writing he could begin to read if only he stared at the wriggling worm long enough. Butch reaches up and slaps himself, then takes out the little spray can, shakes it, and sprays the shit inside it onto the tendril which in an instant freezes solid. The tongs dare him to pluck his own eye out as he grips them in his rubber gloved hand and uses them to grab the frozen tentacle tip and drop it into a jar which he seals up and carries to his attaché case.

The puddle of black goo tries to trickle-crawl away as he sucks it up with a little battery powered wet/dry vac. The shrill whine of the vacuum provokes the nearly inaudible chorus of whispering voices to crescendo into a clamorous babble which makes Butch for the briefest of moments contemplate jamming his thumbs into ears until they puncture his ear drums.

Once all his gear is in the case he gives the bathroom a last once over. Everything looks in order.

"Please mister, please, please kill me," the record skip stripper pleads as Butch emerges from the bathroom.

He locks the door behind him.

"Please . . . please . . . please," the stuck in a loop stripper dancing to the skipping record begs.

He whirls around, pulls his gat, and unloads the magazine into her torso.

Then he sits down at the bar and signals the redneck to pour his second complimentary shot of rotgut.

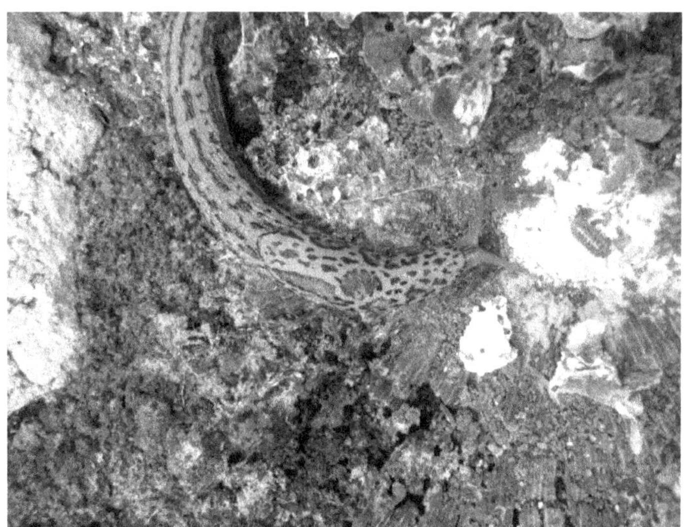

Joshua Dobson is the inventor of the theory (but as of yet not the actual recipe) for the Lemon-Vanilla Marinade a tricky blend of an acid and a base which if ever achieved in actuality will redefine flavor.

Art by Esme

Snuff

By
Madeline White

The pain hit Whiplash like the time she'd caught a knife to the side in a brawl a few years back. Then, she was seventeen, newly minted as an Enforcer in the Shadow Brotherhood, and when the goon with the crown tattooed above his eye slipped his blade between her ribs, she was scared shitless she was going to die. Now, she was twenty-one, clutching the counter in the kitchen to ground herself, and she wished it was a knife.

"Hey, you okay?" Tito asked, looking up from his cutting board full of onions mid-obliteration. Whiplash was supposed to be helping him with dinner, but she hadn't lifted a finger. The Boss may have benched her when she started to show, but she was an Enforcer, not a fucking housewife. And just because babies were rarer than happiness in this nuked-out hellhole didn't mean she was gonna throw away everything she'd ever worked for over one.

"I'm *fine*," she snarled. The blood was between her legs now. Just a little, but no one who has bled in their pants before forgets the feeling.

Another sharp stab of pain almost took her breath away.

Tito wasn't buying it. She could tell he wasn't buying it. Her fingernails turned white as she pressed them into the stained and scarred wood of the countertop. She felt like her insides were being clawed out. Like she was a bloated corpse and the daughter she wanted *so badly* was a starving wolf, ripping open her soft belly to munch on her entrails.

She gagged and brought her hand up to her mouth just in time to stop the hot vomit from passing her lips. She forced it back down. Squirming a bit and already turning away, Tito said, "I'm gonna get Pitbull," and hurried from the kitchen.

When the two of them came back through the kitchen door, Pitbull took one look at Whiplash and her face crumpled. Her eyes lingered on her friend for a long, sympathetic moment, then she turned to Tito, all business, "Go make sure we get a room."

Tito disappeared out of the kitchen again. For Whiplash, the sounds of the Brothers gaming in the other room faded behind an ear-splitting ringing before Tito even started to shut them up.

Pitbull hurried over and gathered Whiplash into her arms. Whiplash sagged, starting to shake. For the first time since she was eight years old, she wanted to cry. She locked a whimper behind gritted teeth and let the other woman help her out of the kitchen and down the hall. Blood trickled down her left thigh.

A handful of Brothers were between the women and the stairs, but none of them looked. They were suddenly absorbed in their poker hands, their smokes, the nail-picked rubber coverings on their joysticks. Whiplash didn't see Rampage among them. She told herself that was for the best.

Nobody had a permanent bedroom in the Lodge, besides the Boss of course. The Brothers slept in the halls, mattresses and dressers lining the upstairs walls of the big old house, everyone allotted their own rectangle of space. But the Lodge had been a real house once, and the bedrooms remained; kitted out and rotated through by Brothers when they needed a little privacy. Pitbull hammered on the door to the best room, kicking Prettyboy into the hall with his dick in his hand.

Once the women were alone, all Whiplash's bravado went out of her like air from a balloon. Pitbull helped her stagger to the bathroom where she curled on the floor and started to cry silent, fat tears while Pitbull assembled a nest of towels and blankets on the tile.

When the next wave of pain came, worse this time, Whiplash rolled up onto her knees and elbows and shoved her fist into a scream. Her teeth left red dents in her knuckles.

Pitbull reached over to stroke her hair, collecting it nimbly into a clip to keep it out of Whiplash's already sweaty face. "It's okay, love," she whispered, "you don't have to try to be quiet."

But she did. She'd fought tooth and nail her entire life to make it to head Enforcer status; standing beside Rampage and only below the Boss himself. And the name of that game was strength. She grabbed a handful of the duvet that Pitbull had brought in and screamed into it until she was dizzy.

"Nobody's gonna think less of you, Whip," Pitbull urged. She meant well. She really fucking did. And if it was just screaming, she'd be right. The Shadows respected pain, and if this was a knife, Whiplash could scream. She *wished* it was a knife.

But it wasn't a knife. And everybody was treating her enough like glass as it was. She demanded Pitbull get the piece of leather from the suture kit under the counter and she put it in her mouth and bit down hard.

After this set of contractions passed, Pitbull helped her peel off her blood-soaked jeans, stripping her down and wrapping her in the blankets on the floor. Pitbull slipped out and returned with a bottle of water and a soft fluffy robe for Whiplash to wear. Whiplash raised a blonde brow, and Pitbull cracked a weak smile, "Stole it from Snapper."

The breath of a laugh puffed through Whiplash's nose before the next wave of cramps set her writhing. The door to the bedroom opened again and Cuervo and Spitfire came in, bearing towels, heating pads, ice packs, and a bucket. Spitfire bent and offered Whiplash a handful of pills. She swallowed them without question.

This time when her body clenched she grunted through her teeth, sweat popping out on her brow. Pitbull wiped her face with a damp rag and

Cuervo clasped her hand. Spitfire bent to open her robe and massage her stomach with the heels of his palms, and she let him. Spit had seen them all in their worst moments, and he wouldn't say a word.

Later, when a break in the contractions left her panting and queasy, Cuervo fed her ice cubes and Pitbull asked gently, "Do you want me to get Ram?"

"No!" Whiplash snarled, lurching towards her on pure reflex.

Anyone else would have flinched. But Pitbull just waited for Whiplash to resettle herself in the sweat-soaked blankets and groan her way through another contraction before she said gently, "Don't you think he deserves to know?"

"I think he deserves to rot in hell," Whiplash hissed through her teeth as the blood and liquid gushed down her pale white thighs.

The other Brothers shared a glance, but they didn't push. Nobody wanted to be on Rampage's bad side. The other head Enforcer, his was the kinda name that made even Brothers shit themselves. But so was Whiplash's, and it was her blood on the floor, not Ram's. So instead of going to get him, they stayed.

They stayed as Whiplash paced back and forth across the bathroom, dripping blood and threatening to bite the head off of anyone who suggested she should lay back down.

They stayed as she writhed and cried and bit down so hard on the piece of leather Pitbull gave her that you probably could have identified her dentals off it.

They stayed as the warped and mangled thing that could have—should have—been her daughter came into the world, as violent and broken as the family that would have been hers.

Cuervo took the body away to clean the blood off of her and Pitbull rubbed Whiplash's neck, and Spitfire made sure that nothing had gone wrong besides everything. When he'd satisfied himself that Whiplash would live to terrorize the people of Denton for another day, he quietly excused himself. There was nothing more he could do.

"I wanna see her," Whiplash said. She felt weak and shaky, but her voice was strong.

Across the bathroom, by the shower, Cuervo looked over her shoulder. Her tight-coiled hair was frizzing around her face, and there was a smear of blood under one of her cat-sharp eyes. "Are you sure?" she asked. She wasn't a squeamish woman, but there was a greyness to her bronze skin under the bug-filled halogen. "It's… She's…"

"I wanna see her," Whiplash insisted. She already felt sick. It was like she knew what she would see before Cuervo even brought the little bundle over.

Cuervo and Pitbull looked at each other over the mound of foul laundry they'd piled in the center of the bathroom, but then Cuervo walked over, picking her way through the mess. She was holding the bundle strangely, like she wanted to treat it lovingly, but she didn't want it too close to her. Like someone might hold a kitten with mange, or a bad-smelling grandmother. She cradled it easily in her hands, wrapped in one of the few towels they had that wasn't too badly stained by years of bleach and blood and vomit.

When Whiplash unwrapped the towel, she sucked in her breath.

She was so impossibly small.

Her head was almost bigger than her body, her face so perfectly formed. And she was beautiful—so beautiful. Her skin was smooth and marble-pale where it stretched delicately over the curves of her skull, soft blue shadows settling where her eyes would have grown.

Whiplash hadn't seen a baby before, not even one like this. Living in a place where the poison dust of nuclear war filled every lung and settled into every bone, even the chance at one was seen as a community miracle. No matter who you were.

When Whiplash had realized she was pregnant, even though she knew the threat it posed to her position, she'd been so overjoyed. She'd spent months lounging about the Lodge, letting the other Brothers take all the heavy work and bring her treats, laying her hands on her slowly swelling belly and imagining meeting the person who was growing there. Even the fact it could only be Rampage's hadn't bothered her then. But now it fucking did.

If everyone in the Brotherhood was a piece of shit, Rampage was the whole muckheap. His knuckles were always bleeding from being cut on somebody's teeth, and his nose was always bleeding from the shit he snorted. He was reckless and impulsive, barrelling through life like a bull in a sea of waving red. Worse than that, he was rotten through and through.

Whiplash had created this perfect little girl with this perfect little face. She grew her in her own body. Nurtured her with her own nutrients, protected her with her own sacrifices. She'd turned the other cheek to every condescending look from the Brothers, resisted her restlessness every time the Enforcers went out, and turned up her nose at every substance she was supposed to. She'd done absolutely everything to make her body a home for this creature, this little person growing inside her.

All Rampage had had to do was contribute something halfway decent. All he'd had to do was be the half that didn't kill her before she had a chance to live. And he'd failed.

Rampage with his rotten soul and his rotten body and his rotten fucking jizz that apparently couldn't produce anything better than the shitbird it came out of.

Because, under her beautiful, perfectly forming little face, Whiplash's daughter was *impossible*. Not something she could have saved by managing her nicotine a little bit better, or sitting out that last brawl when her period was two days late and she didn't think a thing of it. Not a person slipped through her grasp, but a wretched mess of twisted pieces that could have never fit together into something alive.

Her guts were a coiled jumble of deep pink, like worms rushing to feed on her tiny corpse. They weren't on the inside but hanging freely, already starting to dry out and harden. Her arms curled under her chin like she was sleeping, but her legs were nonexistent; stumps terminating under the mess of intestines.

Whiplash felt like she was gonna be sick, and forced it down with the brutal efficiency of long practice. Cuervo hovered nervously above her, watching her reaction. Pitbull looked tactfully away.

For one, two, three long breaths Whiplash looked at her daughter and let herself feel the horror—the unfairness—of all of it.

One breath to grieve the pathetic little creature who would never open her eyes to see the sun, or feel the exhilaration of a punch well landed, or crack open a beer around a bonfire with her friends.

One breath to mourn the life she had imagined for herself while that little soul was growing inside her; a nice quiet house in Denton with a bed that wasn't a pallet on the floor, and a sense of purpose that didn't come with a black crow stamped on the hilt of a switchblade.

One breath to accept that, now that everyone knew her body could do this, she would have to fight twice as hard for the things she'd had before, and that if there was ever a choice between her and Rampage for a job, the Boss would pick Ram every time.

Then she set the little bundle down and gently folded the corners of the towel over the tiny body. She stood up, waving off Pitbull's attempts to help. Her legs trembled, but they held her. No matter what else happened in this world, she'd always been able to count on that.

"Get rid of it," she said to Cuervo.

Cuervo swallowed, her lean throat bobbing as she looked at the bundle on the floor. "Uh…" Her voice was hoarse, and she cleared it. "What did you want me to do with her?"

"I don't care," Whiplash said, even though she did. She wanted to ask that someone find her a coffee can. That's what Brothers were always buried in—ever since the grim days of the Revolution, when that was all they'd had to hold the ashes. It was a tradition, a badge of honor to remind everyone that the Brotherhood had been noble, once. Part of

something bigger than petty crime and shaking down poor saps for protection money. Even though they joked it away, said, "live in a bottle, die in a can", they were all proud of it, deep down.

Whiplash wanted to ask Cuervo to get a good one and make sure it was clean and bury the baby in the side yard with the rest of the Brotherhood. Because she would have been a Brother, if she'd grown up. But she didn't ask for any of that. Instead she walked to the shower and got in like she didn't give a shit.

She let the water pummel her until it ran clear and tepid down the drain. She felt like she should be crying, but nothing came. She was spent, wrung out, empty. Her skin felt loose on her body and she pinched her belly and rolled her flesh between her fingers like she'd never seen it before.

When she got out, Pitbull had cleaned the bathroom. Everything was picked up, the blood wiped away and the floor looking shinier than it had in all the years Whiplash had lived in the Lodge. The bundle was gone like it had never come into this world at all.

Dripping water on the filthy carpet, Whiplash hobbled gingerly to the bed. Something she didn't want to think about dripped down her legs. She felt fucking wretched.

Pitbull lifted the covers for her and then curled around her, like Whiplash wasn't broken and disgusting. Her body was firm and reassuring against Whiplash's back. Her arms were the only thing keeping Whiplash from flying apart into a million pieces.

After a very long time, Pitbull said into Whiplash's neck, "You know that even if you don't tell him, he's gonna find out."

Whiplash knew. Respect and discretion would get her further than most, but there were some secrets that couldn't stay under wraps long, and this was one of them.

She wished desperately that she'd never made it far enough for her body to betray what was going on inside of it. She wished she'd slept with more people in the time when it would have mattered, so that even if the baby had been Rampage's neither of them would have known. Mostly she wished she was still pregnant and that her daughter was alive.

"Fuck him," she said. But there wasn't any feeling in it. There wasn't any feeling in *her*. She'd bled it all out on the bathroom floor.

Pitbull held her close and snuggled into her neck and didn't tell her she was being cruel, even though they both knew she was.

Whiplash felt a sob run through her, soundless and unbidden. Just one. She would not break. Not like this.

"I just hate him so much," she finally breathed into the dead-silent room. It wasn't a secret—she and Rampage had hated each other since she was eight and he was ten and they both realized that the Boss wasn't the kind of man with enough love to go around. But here, rasped past a throat rough from choking back screams, it felt like a confession.

Pitbull didn't say anything to this, not at first. Pitbull was Whiplash's best friend, but she'd never subscribed to the idea that loving Whiplash meant she had to hate everyone Whiplash did. Which was probably good, because Whiplash hated most people.

When she did finally speak, Whiplash expected her to say something gently chastising; to try to get Whiplash to understand that Ram hadn't wanted this, either. That, even though their daughter had been conceived drunkenly in a mutually regretted hate-fuck, he'd done all he could to love her since he found out she existed. To the extent he could love anyone.

But instead Pitbull said, "You know you could still leave. If you wanted to."

Whiplash was so shocked she felt like she'd been kicked in the guts again. She scrambled up, wincing, and stared wide-eyed at the other woman. "What the fuck?" she demanded. "Why would you even say that to me?"

Pitbull was unfazed. She propped herself on an elbow and looked at Whiplash levelly. "You know the Boss would let you retire. He wouldn't like it, but he'd let you. You could move out. Get a nice place downtown. Try again." She chewed her bottom lip before adding, "I'd go with you, when I could."

Whiplash shook her head, still unable to believe what she was hearing, "Pitbull, you *know* how hard I've worked for this, you…"

"I know you work harder than anyone in this place," Pitbull interrupted. "And I know that you still come in behind him, every time, no matter how bad he fucks up. And you always will."

Her words stung, not because they were out of line, but because they were true. Brought into the Shadows two years earlier than her, when he was just six years old, Rampage had always been the Boss's favorite. The Boss said he loved Whiplash, too, but he was a gotdamn liar.

"That doesn't mean I should give up and let him have it," Whiplash retorted. She sank back into the pillows, grimacing and trying to rearrange herself in a way that made her body stop thinking about the fact she'd been turned inside out.

"It's not about him. Either of them. It's about you. And me." Pitbull ran a light finger over the skin of Whiplash's arm, making her shudder. "You have a ticket out. We don't have to *be* here. We don't have to *live like this.*"

She gestured at the room around them, devoid of anything that would mark it as one person's and not a shared resource. The wall was grey-brown around the lightswitch from so many years of unwashed hands pawing for it. There was a rusty stain on the floor big enough for three people to stand in if they were dumb enough to want to. And Whiplash knew Pitbull didn't just mean the room, but the whole Lodge, the whole life they'd built around themselves. All just as crowded and as filthy and as stained with bad memories as this room.

If you swore your oath to the Shadow Brotherhood—cut your palm and took a new name—it wasn't something you could back out of. You could retire at thirty, if you lived that long, or you could break your oath and hope you made it out of the country before they found you, but that was about it. Unless you could have a baby. Then you were free to go.

"I don't want to go," Whiplash said, and she meant it. Even after everything. Even knowing what was still to come. She jutted her chin. "This is my home. My family. This is the life I want."

If Whiplash didn't know Pitbull better, she would have thought this hurt her. For just an instant, something like heartbreak passed through her dark brown eyes. But then her wide mouth split into the toothy grin that was her namesake, and she reached over to tousle Whiplash's blonde hair, just because she knew Whiplash hated it.

"Good. I just wanted to make sure." Her voice was light as a lie, and her fingers lingered a moment too long.

Whiplash remembered the dream she'd had when she first learned she was pregnant, where she wore bright colors instead of a mandated black jacket, and maybe planted flowers in the side yard instead of headstones. She'd been terrified, thinking about it, but excited, too. Like a curtain that had been pulled shut her whole life had suddenly slid open. It was so brief, but the glow of it was blinding.

Whiplash sat up in bed and lit herself a cigarette. It felt good to have it in her fingers after months of getting her nicotine from a patch on her arm. "It's not ideal, but it's safer for the baby than quitting cold turkey," the doctor had said.

Smoke spewed from Whiplash's thin, sharp mouth when she spoke. "I'm a Shadow, Pitbull. Through and through. I'm not gonna let an overdue period change that." She spat the words so they didn't sting her mouth on the way out, and Pitbull crumpled inward a little bit. Whiplash knew she was hurting her, but she couldn't seem to stop. "I know it's a fucking circus, but it's my fucking circus, yeah? And damn it, I'm gonna run this shit one day if I have to shoot Rampage through the skull myself and pry it from his cold, dead hands."

Before Pitbull could say anything, there was a knock on the door. It was polite, but somehow not tentative. A knock that didn't hammer, didn't demand to be heard, but made no apology for being there. The women exchanged a glance, Whiplash nodding her permission before Pitbull slipped out of bed to get the door.

It was Rampage. He wasn't crying, but his knuckles were bleeding, which for him was the same thing.

He had brought her a coffee can.

Madeline White is a queer farmer, artist, and New Yorker, who knows a dystopia when she sees one and wants to be the first to write about it. Her work has been published in a variety of magazines and anthologies, including Honeyguide Magazine (Issue 8), Flash Fiction Online (June 2025 issue), and What if We Kissed While Sinking a Billionaire's Yacht by Not A Pipe Publishing. When she's not writing, you can find her hanging out with her horse or exploring the country in her box truck "RV".

Art by Mike David

My Correspondence with the Goat Man

By
Jon Clendaniel

Dear Goat Man,

I'm glad I'm finally here. That bus ride sucked. When they said this place was in the middle of nowhere, they meant it.

I'm pretty sure Mom and Dad picked the furthest summer camp they could find. They must still be mad about the incident with the curtains. They're probably laughing at me right now while sipping old fashioneds on the back porch.

I'll be sleeping in one of the camp's sketchy old cabins. I have seven roommates. The kid in the bunk above me smells like cabbage. It's not ideal.

I wish you could've come with me, but I guess you have to stay in one place. "Spatially locked," I think is how you put it.

On the bright side, I found a closet where I can practice my rituals without being interrupted. I got some weird looks when I unpacked my candles and my robe. One kid, Connor, wished me a happy Halloween.

Oh, by the way, thanks for teaching me how to do a "Sending" (is that what it's called?). It feels kind of old school, like writing a letter, except with extra steps. I almost forgot to put those symbols in the corner of the parchment.

This place seems like it'll be boring as—I was going to say Hell, but from what you've told me, Hell is anything but boring. Maybe I can practice some of those incantations you taught me. Otherwise, it's gonna be a long two weeks.

Sincerely yours,

Billy

Dear Billy,

Good to hear from you, kiddo! I'm glad you've mastered the art of Sending. I think of it like email, but more elegant.

Things aren't quite the same here without you. I'm going to miss our evening chats, your good-natured humor, your unique insights on mortal life. And, of course, scaring the shit out of you.

In your absence, I've decided to begin haunting your little sister, Christy. Seeing as she's only four, I expect it won't be too difficult.

Re: incantations—by all means, keep practicing! Just be sure to keep away from anything flammable. We don't want you flambéing any more curtains. And remember what I've always said, it's all about *presentation*.

Sincerely,

G-Man

Dear Goat Man,

I think I might have made a bad first impression.

We were telling spooky stories around the campfire. The other kids took turns telling the usual stuff—ghosts, haunted houses, alien abductions, slenderman, et cetera. Ooh, I'm terrified.

Then it was my turn. I remembered the stories you told me about your home. I figured I'd adapt a few of them, change the names, maybe exaggerate a bit for dramatic effect.

Hoo boy. I honestly didn't expect so much crying. Who knew a little cosmic horror and existential dread could upset kids so badly? The one about your old friend Beelzebub really set them off. A bunch of kids ran away to their bunks. At least three peed themselves.

Now the kids give me even weirder looks than before. And I'm not allowed to tell campfire stories anymore.

Sincerely yours,

Billy

Dear Billy,

Don't worry about those kids—they clearly can't appreciate the finer points of the demon realm.

I have begun the process of terrifying Christy. It is not going well. She does not respond to the traditional methods. I've popped out of the closet, jumped out from under the bed… I've even taken the form of her favorite teddy bear, spinning its head around and winking at her. Nothing.

Usually she smiles and waves at me. Once, she appeared to flip me off (I wonder where she learned that, young man!). Last night, she even giggled at me. *At me*, a chief demon of the fifth level! You wound me, Christy.

Clearly, I must change my approach. This shouldn't be this difficult.

Sincerely,

Your Favorite Sleep Paralysis Demon

Dear Goat Man,

I went kayaking today. My friends Connor, Mike, and Vicky challenged me to a race.

The current carried us around the bend to where the creek widens. When we were out of sight of the rest of the kids, we started playing a game called "bumper boats." You play bumper boats by ramming your kayak into other people's kayaks. I got the worst of it. My friends teamed up on me, bumping into my kayak from either side, rocking it back and forth. I have to admit, it was kind of fun. We were all laughing it up when my kayak got tipped over.

I was upside down in the water, jerking my body around, trying to flip myself upright. Wishing I had done more of those ab workouts Mr. Hodak showed us in gym class. Eventually, I gave up on flipping the kayak and tried to wriggle my body free from the boat. Gross creek water flooded into my nose, reminding me of when I snorted chocolate milk in the cafeteria last year. I must say, I preferred the chocolate milk.

Somehow, I worked my legs free of the kayak and swam to the surface. After I finished gasping for air, I looked around and saw that my friends were gone. They must've gotten called back to the dock while I was underwater.

Later, I ran into them in the cafeteria. They asked how I liked playing bumper boats. I told them I still had water in my ears. We all had a good laugh about it. Mike said it "builds character," whatever that means.

Sincerely yours,
Billy

Dear Billy,
Bumper boats sound a lot like a game we played in my youth, on the Styx.

I'm glad you're making some human friends.

Things have been quiet here. When I haven't been unsuccessfully haunting Christy, I've spent my nights exploring the house. Man, your parents' TV is nice. I was flipping through the channels and I came across one of those "televangelists" of yours. I remembered seeing his name on a list back home. The Big Man Downstairs has something special planned for him when the time comes. Fire and brimstone, indeed.

I've also taken the liberty of sampling your parents' wine collection. It is superb. Though I typically prefer beverages with a higher haemoglobin content, if you catch my drift. The merlot, in particular, pairs well with live animal sacrifices. On a related note, sorry about the cat. You know me, I get hangry.

Sincerely,
The G.O.A.T. Man

Dear Goat Man,
It's okay about the cat. I never liked it anyway.

We went on a hike today. The counselors had us split up into groups of four. Connor, Mike, and Vicky picked me for their group.

We were walking through the woods for a while, I'm not sure how long, when we spotted a tunnel in a hillside just off the path. Must've been part of an abandoned mine or something. My friends dared me to go down it. Vicky said she'd hug me if I did. I couldn't say no.

I walked down the tunnel for a little while, tripping over rocks and debris. I guess I should've been scared, but compared to the stuff you've shown me, this was nothing. I called to my friends a couple times, and they encouraged me to keep going.

I could hardly see anything by the time I got to the end of the tunnel. It was just a big pile of rocks. How disappointing.

When I came out of the tunnel, there was no one there.

I figured it out—I'd been pranked! I couldn't help laughing. Oh boy, they got me good! Sending me on a wild goose chase and then running off. Brilliant!

Then I realized I had no idea where I was.

The forest next to the camp is pretty big. It goes on for miles, getting thicker and darker the further you go. Even though I was on the trail, it took me hours to find my way back to camp. I think I took a couple wrong turns when the path forked.

It was dark when I got back. The counselors yelled at me for scaring them to death. If a kid being gone for a few hours is enough to scare them to death, remind me not to introduce them to you.

I saw Mike and Connor on my way back to the cabins. They grinned at me, and I smiled back. "Good one!" I called. They laughed and went inside their cabin.

I was too excited to sleep tonight. I lay in my bunk, ignoring the smell of cabbage from above, going over the spells you taught me and plotting ways to get back at my friends.

I can't wait for tomorrow.

Sincerely yours,

Billy

Dear Billy,

Ah, the joys of pranks! Makes me nostalgic for my own youth, all those aeons ago.

I'm sure you'll come up with something good for your friends. But please, nothing like the stunt you pulled on Mr. Meeks from down the street last year.

Christy has made passing remarks about her friend "Go-Man" to your parents. Believing me to be her imaginary friend, they smile and pat her head and then return to their mundane prattling. Their obtuseness makes me wish I could haunt them, instead. If only I could manifest to adults! Alas, the adult mind is clouded with worldly concerns, leaving no room for my kind to slip in.

Enjoy your unencumbered young mind while you can, my friend.

Sincerely,

Goaty McGoatface

Dear Goat Man,

I got up early today so I could perform my morning incantations to prep for today's pranks. Speaking of which, I'm glad no one's stumbled upon my closet yet. If someone saw a pentagram on the floor with all those runes and candles and stuff, there'd be a lot of awkward questions.

After breakfast we went fishing at the pond. I remembered Vicky talking about how much she wanted a nose piercing, so I had her give herself one with a fishhook. A simple mind control spell, only enough to last a few seconds, but it got the job done. I'm sure her parents will love her new look.

In the afternoon we went to the archery range. It was a lot of fun, especially when I made Connor wander in front of the targets while the counselors weren't looking. Good thing Mike's such a terrible shot, otherwise Connor would have a hole in his head instead of his lower thigh. Those arrowheads are sharper than you think.

I saw my three friends at the campfire tonight. They looked pretty scared. When they were roasting marshmallows, they seemed afraid that they would explode in their hands. As if I would stoop that low.

If only they knew what I have planned for them next.

Sincerely yours,

Billy 

Dear Billy,

Saw Mr. Meeks today. Good news, he's out of his wheelchair!

I have other good news as well: I finally scared your sister.

Here's how I did it.

I waited until she was almost asleep. Drifting off into dreamland, but still tethered to the waking world. That's where I thrive. But you already know that. Anyway, as her eyes were fluttering shut, I leaned over her, swelling myself up as big as I could get. I took the form of all of her nightmares at once. Stuff I've gleaned from looking into her dreams, prying into her subconscious mind. I tell you, for a four-year-old, there's some wild stuff in there.

I presented myself as a floating tetrahedron, flitting from one horrifying shape to the next in a matter of seconds. There were images of bad experiences—scoldings from your parents, wetting herself in preschool. There were monsters, demons more terrible than myself, formless things characterized only by a vague sensation of dread. Where does she come up with this stuff?

I intensified my shapeshifting and spoke to her in her half-awake state.

Hey, Christy.

Her eyes snapped open.

I then transformed into the scariest monster in her imagination. It was based on a cartoon she saw on a cereal box, of all things. It had wormed its way into her mind and evolved into something beyond terrible, with dripping fangs, razor claws, and a wild mane of dark fur. In the form of the creature, I worked my jaws into a wide grin.

You didn't say goodnight to me, I growled.

She screamed. It was one of those groggy, terrified screams that barely makes any sound, when you're not sure if you're awake or dreaming and you can't move your limbs because I've immobilized them and you just want to cry for help, to make any noise at all, but nothing comes out. I know you know the feeling. When I allowed her to regain full consciousness, she broke out into sobs. I resumed my normal form and stood at the foot of her bed.

Her crying intensified, growing louder. I leaned in, concerned that I may have overdone it. Then she removed her hands from her face, and I could see her mouth was split in a huge smile. She saw me, and her eyes lit up.

"Again! Again!" she shrieked, clapping her hands.

I took a bow. A bravura performance, if I may say so.

Sincerely,

One Baaad Man

Dear Goat Man,

I'm glad you finally got Christy. It might sound cheesy, but I've been wanting to introduce her to you. As her big brother, I feel like I should share stuff with her—in this case, my cool demon friend.

With camp ending in a couple days, I've been busy pranking Connor, Mike, and Vicky.

I tried out that hallucination spell you showed me. I figured, while they were walking around camp and no one else was looking, I'd make them see ghosts. First, I had them see an old lunch lady with an apron and a kitchen knife. Then, I conjured an image of a big dude in a hockey mask (you know how much I love *Friday the 13th*). At some point, I think the spells got crossed up or something, because they started seeing a lady in an apron wearing a hockey mask. Which was probably just as scary, but still. They told the counselors about the ghosts, but of course no one believed them. Now, the other kids go "woo woo" every time one of them walks into a room.

On the second-to-last night, we had a talent show. I had to back out of doing my "magic tricks"—I'd been doing enough spells already!

When Connor, Mike, and Vicky came onstage to sing "Wagon Wheel" (how original), I cast that neat confusion spell you taught me. Turns out, "Wagon Wheel" isn't as catchy when you're speaking in tongues. ("Rock me ghiaoenvk like a daghiopahfioah"—you get the idea). The judges gave them bad scores for showing off.

Then, on the last day, the whole camp played capture the flag.

After we broke up into teams and went into the woods, I put the "lost time" hex on the three of them. While the rest of us ran around tagging each other and having a ball, my three friends went on a little side trip. Hours later, when the game was over, they stumbled out of the woods—clothes torn and filthy, hair all messed up—raving about how they were lost in the forest for days and they never thought they'd see other people again and blah, blah, blah. From the look in their eyes, I could tell they were beyond terrified.

How desperate did they get? Did they eat bugs? Did they drink their own pee? I don't really want to know, but at the same time I kind of do.

After the campfire, when we were walking back to our cabins, I chased them down. I asked them how their walk in the woods went. They were still pretty shellshocked at that point—they just mumbled a bit.

"Good," I said. "You know, stuff like that…"

I then transformed my face briefly into the lunch lady, then Jason V., then settled on yours.

"*…builds character,*" I finished in a deep growl, like the one you used to do when you first started haunting me.

You should've seen their faces. They couldn't believe it was me the whole time! They just stood there, mouths open, looking like they'd just discovered *true* fear for the first time. You know the look.

"Hahaha!" I couldn't contain my laughter. "Gotcha! You guys were so scared!"

They didn't seem to find it funny. I guess pranks, like all humor, are—what did you call it? Subjective, that's the word. Anyway, I told them how much I enjoyed playing our little practical jokes on each other, and guess what? I invited them all for a sleepover next week! They agreed right away. "Anything you want, Billy," they said. They seemed really eager to please me.

I can't wait to introduce them to you and Christy.

Sincerely yours,

Billy

Dear Billy,

Re: the hallucination spell—I think what happened was you mixed up the syntax. It should be "aleph, teth, daleth," not "daleth, aleph, teth." A common mistake—we'll work on it.

What an inventive mix of enchantments you used! You are truly on your way to rivaling the best of the mortal spellsmiths. I'm so proud of you.

Looking forward to seeing you and meeting your new friends! I've been brainstorming with Christy—she's my new "partner in crime." She and I have a special scare planned for you when you get home.

Your Friend,
Goat Man

Jon Clendaniel is a writer of speculative fiction from western Pennsylvania. His work has appeared in *Illustrated Worlds*, *Flash Point Science Fiction*, and *Shelter of Daylight*, among others. When not writing, he can usually be found watching obscure horror movies or buying way too many used paperbacks.

Art by Kit Carter

Thin Man

By

e rathke

He pressed his left temple to her left temple and the nose of the gun to his right temple. Her eyes closed, her breath was even and her heart slow, but his was rapid and shallow. He pulled the trigger.

The Thin Man watched the window shatter and the volcano of gore erupt. He held the hand of a little girl with short, cherry hair. Billy, her stuffed green bunny, hung limply from her other hand. There were no tears, but the gunshot rang in her ears leaving the world muffled and distant.

"Say goodbye to mummy." The Thin Man's voice was faint and jagged.

She did not speak.

They turned and walked away from the house.

"Will I see Mummy and Daddy again?" She clutched Billy tight.

The Thin Man stopped and squatted down before her flooded eyes in which he saw his own reflection. He picked her up and carried her away, her eyes watching the house grow farther and farther away, one step at a time.

She watched him for months, barely breathing, while he prowled through the house, all sinew and bone. Every rib pierced through, sharp hips and shoulder blades like wings. The skin of his head stretched so tight it threatened to rip leaving a skull like chrome. He walked shirtless and shoeless, each step soundless, leaving no footprints. Hands like talons that he rubbed over his baldness, tapped on the walls, and tugged out souls.

"What would you like for breakfast, my dear?" The words pierced her ears and danced up her spine.

"Um," she dropped her eyes to the table then back to his sunken eyes, "eggs."

He nodded and turned to the refrigerator where he collected eggs, an onion, peppers, and cheese. Washing and chopping, whisking and combining with claws of ivory, he tossed it all on a pan and scrambled it together. He hunched over and his vertebrae rose from his skin like the spine of a dragon, jagged and conspicuous. His movements were silent, only the occasional touch of metal spatula to metal pan chimed through the sizzle. His neck craned and his head leaned over his shoulder, snakelike. "Would you like some toast?"

She nodded her head once. The smells collided in her nostrils, and she became hungry.

Slowly, his head returned to its bowed position over the food. He popped in the toast and grabbed a plate, a glass, and a jug of orange juice. The plate was filled with eggs on toast and placed in front of her with a glass of orange juice.

"Thank you."

The Thin Man nodded and handed her a knife and fork. She had never seen him eat and was not surprised by his skeletal figure, but she wondered how he survived. Using only her fork, she cut into the eggs and ate. "These are really good." She meant it, like she always did. The peppers added spice and flavor, the cheese cooled her mouth and calmed her taste buds, and the eggs filled her up.

He wiped his hands on his pants and nodded and sat across from her. "Cut with your knife."

She tried to manage the movements of knife and fork. "I can do it with my fork."

He came behind her, put the knife in her right hand, the fork in her left, and moved her hands for her. "Like this." His hands were delicate and soft, not at all like the claws she envisioned. They stabbed with the fork through the egg and bread, and cut behind it with the knife, freeing a bitesize bit. She ate it. His head came into view, his body wrapped around behind her, and he nodded, smiling with his dark eyes. He returned to his seat and watched her eat.

The house was wood with one floor containing five rooms, a kitchen, two bedrooms, a sitting room, and his always locked room. She wandered through the woods that surrounded the house with her green bunny, playing tag with the trees, mimicking the birds, and lying in the grass watching the clouds float by and teaching the bunny what they were made of. The piano mingled with the chirping of the robins and blue jays, the rustling of squirrels, and the cascade of crickets. He played slow melodic songs, minimal in movement, and repetitive in nature that lasted for hours. Her time passed in eighth and sixteenth notes, punctuated by the hours-long breaks he would take to wander the woods with her, the bunny always in hand. He gave her the names and songs of birds, taught her to climb trees and speak to squirrels. He spoke sparingly, barely a handful of words a day passed between them; their life contained in their stretch of forest like a bubble forgotten by the world where nature flourished. Deer roamed often and they did not fear the Thin Man, nor could they hear him move. She feared their size at first, but he brought one to her and showed their gentleness. He wandered with them through the woods and sat whispering with squirrels. An endless summer, the sun always shined, and the grass was always green, the flowers always in bloom. By day, he taught her the notes of the keys and the letters of words. They farmed and tended the chickens. When he was away, she taught her bunny all that she learned. At night, he told her stories of princesses and goblins, dragons, and knights, stories of a beauty and a beast, of children lost in the woods and trapped in a house of gingerbread. She studied him in the moonlight, the shadows heavy from the many contours of his body. His eyes abyssed and his silhouette disappeared. He was there, but she could

see through him. She touched his hand to make sure
he was real and he held on until she slept.

"Sleep well, my dear."

He then retreated to the locked room.

They stood outside of a large house. The top
floor was lit, but the bottom lay dark. His hand was
hot on hers and she clutched her green bunny tightly
to her chest.

"Wait here, my dear."

"Where are we?"

He dropped to one knee, patted her on the
head with a smile, his ivory squared teeth glimmered,
and he walked toward the house wearing the charcoal
pants he always wore. The door opened before him
and closed behind. She looked all around her at the
trees that surrounded the house and the cul-de-sac
twenty feet back. The driveway was a backwards "h"
allowing for many cars. She counted the windows
viewable from the front, which numbered ten. A car
drove by like a wisp, the sound elliptical in
magnitude, which was swallowed once again by the
hum of streetlights. The birds did not sing here, and
the animals were aloof. It unsettled her, and she
spoke to her bunny, "It's okay, Billy. He'll be back
soon." She sat on the steps in front of the house
facing the street and the lonely light that washed the
gate with color.

A gunshot fired and she jumped to her feet,
hugging Billy the Bunny. It was like the world spun
out, toppled off balance. The lights flicked off in the
house and she backed away, looking all round her. It
returned then, an action she had no words for,
something years old, before the trees and songs. Only

Billy remembered that far back and she looked into
his doll eyes, which were touched by a single yellow
spot of light. The door opened and the Thin Man
walked towards her.

He reached one hand for her to take. She
looked from the hand to Billy and back to the hand.
For once, Billy was silent and her heart raced faster.

"What is the matter, my dear?"

She took his hand and they walked from the
house down the street and into the woods.

She knocked on the locked door, clutching
Billy. The door opened quickly, but it was too dark in
the house to see.

"What is it, my dear?"

"I had a bad dream." Her throat ached, and
her voice filled with tears.

He squatted and opened his arms for
embrace. She hugged him tightly, clinging to him
with Billy hanging over his back. Picking her up, he
brought her back to her bed, but she did not let go,
so they both lied down. "Tell me about your dream."

Her face was so close to him that she could
smell him for the first time. It was faint, but he
smelled like earth and fire, but the fire was far away,
smoldering. "There was a man and a woman. Billy
said they were Mummy and Daddy. We were
swimming, but then a big black bird came and it
swooped down really fast and they couldn't get away
and it was so big that I couldn't see the sun anymore
and it stole them right out of the water and I
screamed for them as loud as I could but they
couldn't get away from the big bird and I wanted to
go with them but the bird wouldn't come back. It just

left me alone in the water and I cried and then I woke up."

"There are no black birds here, my dear."

"I wish I could be with my parents."

"You'd be dead."

"I know."

"Do you want to die?"

Her forehead knit. "I want to be with Mummy and Daddy."

"You will see them again one day and they will be glad."

"Will it be long?"

"It will seem like it."

She rolled onto her back and stretched her arms to the ceiling, holding Billy above her. "I don't remember them so good, but Billy does. He remembers everything."

"He's a very smart bunny."

She hugged Billy and closed her eyes.

"Would you like to hear a story?"

"Mhm."

"Once there was a princess who lived in this forest. She had long red hair like fire and could talk to all the animals that lived here. The birds sang for her and the playful deer danced for her. She loved them so much that she wanted to make sure they would never suffer. Singing to the spirits of the trees and the lord of the skies, she asked that the sun would always shine and flowers would always bloom. She told them that if they didn't make it so, she would leave the forest forever and the sun would follow her because of her pure soul. You see, she was ageless, but always like a child in curiosity and generosity. The spirits fell in love with her and all adored each note she sang, so they promised to never let the forest die, not even for a winter. The sun became tied to her and only slept when she did, but the sun sent the moon always to watch her sleep and make sure no evil befell her. The forest flourished and roses blossomed in her footsteps. She loved this place, far away from the world, but inside of it. You can still see her magic and hear her song if you listen close to the trees and the birds. That's why I teach you their language."

"Mhm." Her eyes were closed and her breath evened, but she hung onto Billy with both hands.

"Sleep well, my dear."

He left occasionally. Gone before she woke and back after she fell asleep, returning with clothes, books, whatever she asked for. Most of the food she ate came from the forest or the lake or their chickens. When he returned, he appeared brighter and more energetic, his songs sprightlier. She asked him what he did but never received a response. Sometimes he brought her along, leaving her to watch him enter a home and leave several minutes later with the pierce of gunshot ringing through the air. For days afterward, she hid from him. Each day without the Thin Man brought the image of her father and mother clearer, but the shadows remained long. She investigated the house and the grounds in his absence, dancing in the melody of the leaves and the wind, the birds and the squirrels. Nothing was secret to her except the windowless room behind the locked door, the only lock she knew, the only place closed to her.

As she grew older, she no longer needed him to hold her hand or read her stories till she slept.

Lying awake with the moonlight through her window, she tried to recall the voice of her father, the face of her mother, but there was little to find. The Thin Man's face blotted out the past, his voice dragged them from her. The years mounted and she aged, but The Thin Man remained unchanged. With every year, she stepped further from childhood, but his image mirrored the same one she saw so many years before.

A hawk hung in the air, a faint shadow figure-eighting above the earth, edging close to the noon sun. Her hair curled from the end of the dock into the water in fiery rolls. She held Billy above her, matching the movements of the hawk, trying to block it away or wait for Billy to take flight, if only they could get the timing right. The Thin Man cast his lure into the lake, whooshing through the air until it plopped thirty paces out. Flicking the head of the pole back and forth, he reeled it in slow, trying to mimic the movement of a small fish.

"You'll fly one day, Billy boy." She rolled over onto her stomach, her hair wrapped round her, the tip wet and dangling above the surface, and hung Billy over the water, his ears hovering just above the lake.

"You're too old to talk to that bunny." The Thin Man's eyes followed the ripple of water created by his line, his voice faint and sharp as it always was, like a petal afloat in water that could cut through steel.

"I don't have anyone else to talk to."

"You can talk to me, my dear."

"You never speak unless you're teaching me."

He nodded. "The squirrels and deer."

She pulled Billy from the water and pulled her legs underneath her, sitting up. "They're too suspicious, superstitious, and dumb."

His reeling hesitated for a moment and he looked at her. Her bright green eyes were large and almond shaped. "Squirrels are smarter than humans. You criticize them unfairly, my dear. One afternoon the right squirrel will teach you all that you'll ever need to know."

She dropped to her back, her legs still crossed, and sighed. Her arm over her face, blocking the sun, she watched his caged back. He cast no shadow.

He returned his attention to the lake. Fishless, he recast.

"Do fish talk?"

"Not to me."

She got up, removed her shorts and shirt and dove naked into the water. Reappearing, she spit water in an arch and pulled her hair back. Looking back at the Thin Man, his image distorted in the light like a phantom. He barely took up space and the light swallowed him. She swam further out into the lake.

"Be careful of the line." His voice was right over her shoulder, like he whispered it to her, but she did not look back.

She pulled on his line and turned to him. He stood motionless, patient like the dock. She had never seen him hurry, never seen him panic. His movements were imperceptible, silent, and forgotten. He frightened her, even still, after ten years, like a ghost that her life revolved around. She dove into the water as deep as she could. The fish avoided her and the water became cold and murky and she could swim no deeper. Arriving back to the surface, the

Thin Man was gone. Floating on her back, the hawk flew back and forth across the sky. The wind carried piano keys over the water, and the years fell away behind her eyelids.

She was tired of the endless summer and the forest. She had never seen the leaves change or the snow fall, only read of them. It rarely rained, but the growth never abated. The sun washed over her and browned her skin.

She knocked on the locked door, letting Billy hang from one hand. The house was dark and when he opened the door, she could not see past him. He was only a head taller than her, but he seemed smaller.

"What is it, my dear?"

"Can't sleep."

He stepped out of the room and closed the door behind him. "Why?"

"I don't know. I keep thinking about my parents." She could not see his face, but she imagined he frowned.

"You do not want to die, do you?"

"No." Her eyes fell to her feet, and she pulled Billy into her arms. "I just wish I could remember them."

He nodded.

"I can't remember their faces or voices. There's only this place and you." Her eyes raised to his black holes.

"I'm sorry, my dear." He placed a hand on her shoulder.

"Will you stay with me till I fall asleep, like you used to?"

He nodded. She took his hand and they walked back to her room. She got in bed, but he sat in the chair beside it, like he did when reading to her as a child.

"Get in." She patted the bed.

He climbed in and lay next to her. He smelled like earth and ember, the same as ten years before. She sidled up next to him and lay her head on his chest. Hard and bony, like a birdcage, but warm, a fire burned inside. She kept it there to listen to his heart, but she heard nothing. He stroked her hair and held her loose, but she gripped him tight to make him real.

"Your heart doesn't beat." She lifted her head and looked him in the eyes.

He said nothing.

"Do you have a heart?"

"I have all that I need here."

She rested against his chest once more. "Why did you take me here?"

"I couldn't leave you there."

She closed her eyes and tried to remember that night, but all that came was the gunshot. His chest did not raise and fall with the act of breathing.

They stayed there, unmoving, enveloped by the dark amid a forest that never wilted. She ran her finger along one of his ribs, traced it to his wrist, which was like a twig in her hand, thin, but hard as stone. His hand caressed her head, running through her hair.

"I don't even know your name. I call you Thin Man in my head or when I talk to Billy, but you're the only person I know. You're the only person I can see when I close my eyes, but, sometimes, you don't even feel real. Like, if I tried, I could see through you or make you disappear, like a bad dream." She raised her head to look at him again. "You're my whole life."

He did not move or speak. His eyes were blacked out in the dark like caverns. She could see nothing in them.

"I love you and I don't even know you."

"You're just a child yet."

"I know what I feel."

"You cannot love me."

"But I do." She clung to him and pressed her face into his neck. "I love you."

He separated from her, but she knew not how. She fell into her pillow and he sat on the bed beside her, his eyes out the window. She lay there, confused and spurned. Her heart raced, the air caught in her throat, and spiders crawled under her skin, up her spine.

"Did my dad own a gun?" She wavered, like she was falling through the floor.

He did not look at her. "I don't know."

"Why do you do it?"

"It must be done."

"But why him? Why them?" She broke and tears flung from her face, blotting her vision.

He came from behind and held her.

Her chest heaved and her voice collapsed. "I hate you and this place." She struggled to free herself and he let her go. "Why do you keep me here?"

He took her hand and held it. His face appeared through the darkness, his eyes closed, and his eyebrows upturned. He kissed her hand. "I'm sorry, my dear."

She flung her arms around him and cried.

"Sleep well, my dear."

"Goodnight."

He stood for a moment longer and slipped from the room.

She waited half an hour, or what she believed to be half an hour, then crept out her window. The moon shown bright and she sighed, blowing her bangs out of her eyes. The grass was soft and slightly wet from the late sprinkle of rain. Clouds spread like fingers over the star filled sky. The trees were silent and she walked towards them, rubbing a hand on the bark of each one she passed. The squirrels were all off gathering nuts or fighting the birds for space, so they were occupied as well. She found some flint and grabbed the fallen branches she had collected and the leaves she dried. The walk back to the house weighed on her steps and she heard them, like she was empty as a cave and each step was a drop of water into a pool. Her life fell away, the twelve years she spent in the forest with the Thin Man, the languages, the lessons, the books. A prisoner ready to be freed. A child ready to start a life. A lover spurned. She was hollow, as hollow as he, with his heartless, lungless chest. If cracked open, she was sure she would find only the bones that shown so clear beneath his thin layer of flesh. Through the door, her steps were soft, the things he taught used against him. She built a pyre before the locked door with the leaves, twigs, and branches. In her room, she grabbed Billy, for there was no life without him. As quietly as possible, she struck the flint and started the fire.

She sat outside beneath the stars and the moon watching the house catch light and burn. The smoke plumed towards the stars, and she connected a line from Orion to the black smoke. The fire leapt

higher and higher, a dance of orange, red, and yellow. Demons lapping at the dark, swallowing it and growing larger, consuming everything. She smiled taking in the heat of the night. The music of the forest came dissonant, the animals fleeing the area, the fire crescendoing with cracks and snaps of wood and the roar of current rushing through the blaze. Lying back, she caught sight of a shooting star and traced it with Billy.

"We're going to have a real life now." She hugged him and smiled, the first smile in a long time, longer than she could remember.

A roar ripped through the flames, different than the one the funeral pyre made. She sat up.

A shadow emerged from the flames. It stretched its arms wide towards the heavens and screamed, stabbing out the discordant chords of fire and nature. It stepped towards her, hazed in the heat and black as soot. Falling to its knees, it rubbed a taloned hand over its skull.

With each step, the image of the Thin Man grew fainter and fainter.

e rathke writes about books and games at radicaledward.substack.com. A finalist for the Baen Fantasy Adventure and recipient of the Diverse Worlds Grant, he is the author of Glossolalia, the lofi cyberpunk series Howl, and the space opera series The Shattered Stars. His short fiction appears in Queer Tales of Monumental Invention, Mysterion Magazine, Shoreline of Infinity, and elsewhere.

Art by Esme

The Money Left in the Account

By
Jennifer Jeanne McArdle

There's 2631 euros left in this bank account, and I just want to remember what my damn pin is so I can get the rest of my money and go home.

The truth is it's not something *I* can remember because I never knew what the pin was; my other head, my sister, used to take care of this kind of stuff. But she's dead now, and her head and neck have been removed, and the bones of my sternum and my shoulder have been rearranged to make it look like I've only ever had one head, but my right shoulder still is longer than my left and sloped downward in a way that makes me looked crooked and not capable of playing any sport, let alone baller bat, which is what my sister and I used to play and the source of the money I can't get out of this account.

6 numbers. I guessed the pin she used for her cell phone. The machine beeps its disappointment.

When I was in high school, the gym teacher called all the conjoined twins and asked us to meet her on the field behind the school. There were just six of us in the whole school. In the past, it would be unheard of to have any conjoined twins at a high school, but now, with all the radiation poisoning along with better healthcare, more conjoined twins are born (and surviving) each year.

6 more numbers. Mom's birthday. My sister always liked my mom. I liked my dad. Again, it's a no go. The ATM sounds annoyed this time although I know it doesn't remotely care, which makes this even more frustrating.

The gym teacher gave us some large flat bats, helmets (one for each head), and conjoined twins, adult men with two heads, sauntered over to us in designer athleisure, crossed their arms, and scrutinized the raggedy group of children sitting in the grass. We struggled to understand the accent of the head on the right as he explained the rules of baller bat, a hugely popular game overseas in which all the players are conjoined twins. "Mr. and Mr. Klaus are talent scouts. If you can impress them, you may get offered a spot on one of the most popular and successful baller bat teams in the European League."

The day Ruffy died. Ruffy was the cat my sister had; it liked her better than it liked me. That date didn't work either, and I'm nervous that if I put in another wrong number I'm going to get locked out, and then I'll have to talk to someone in the bank, which I am trying to avoid. I don't feel like being recognized or pitied.

Me and my sister were really good at baller bat. Once we graduated high school, the Mr. Klauses recruited us to play on a Dutch team. We weren't super famous, but we were well-known amongst sports fans. My sister, being my sister, learned Dutch and gave all the interviews, even though most Dutch people spoke English and didn't seem to care that much about foreign players learning their language. When we played, she was the one who batted the stray balls away (if they hit you, you'd have to freeze for a few moments) while I concentrated on our footwork, just keeping the large, bouncy goal ball dribbling between my feet as we ran and navigated around other players, using my arm to push them away, until we finally made it close enough to kick and score. Dutch people liked my sister, were charmed by her. I was the silent, quiet head, the head that was always eating or biting my lower lip, expressing whatever emotion my sister had trained herself to repress.

I debate using up one more try on an idea I'd had from the beginning of this adventure but was trying to avoid. It is ridiculous, but something compels me. The date of my sister's death. She took her own life. The screen changes, processes, blinks. What do I want to do with my account?

Of course, this is either a huge coincidence or my sister had been planning her death on this date for a long while, for whatever reason. After she shot herself, and I woke up in the hospital bed, people asked me if I'd known she was depressed, suicidal. How could I not have known? Weren't we psychic or the same person, even? We shared nearly every organ, the same DNA, but still, between our brains might as well have been an ocean of distance. She never told me she wanted to die. They held a funeral ceremony. A charity funded the reconstructive surgery needed for my shoulder. I recovered in the hospital, watched my former baller bat team lose game after game. I failed at giving compelling interviews, even in English, and then weeks passed, and without the charm of my second head, folks seemed to quietly move on from my sister. From me. From the tragedy of star players' careers cut so short in their prime.

The machine spits out almost all the money, but it doesn't carry small bills, so my last 11 euros are stuck in this account forever, unless I get the courage to close the account out in person, which would probably be the smart thing to do because I can't be a baller bat player again, and I won't live in the Netherlands again, and I probably won't live in another part of Europe.

Probably. But who can say—there's an ocean between my mind now and my mind years from now. No one really knows what their future self will want, especially because that self will be alone, a single head for one body, for the first time. For now, the crisp, colorful bills in my hand feel soothing, like lotion, like a mystical balm.

I suppose I really did know enough about her, in the end.

Jennifer writes speculative shorts and lives in New York where she works in animal conservation. Her website: https://jenniferjeannemcardle.blogspot.com/

Art by Kit Carter

The Butcher of Mazdin

By
Shantell Powell

The Butcher of Mazdin towers high atop his pedestal, a bronze monument huge enough to empty all the mines in the region. Every seven years, we throng to his feet in the heat of the solstice to make offerings. All must make blood offerings when the sun is at its zenith, and all must wear white—even babes in arms. There are no exceptions. To give white garments to paupers is a sacrament. The richest of us give ceremonial robes to the poorest and are lauded for their generosity. I have given nothing.

The richest bring cattle, but most bring something less extravagant. A goat, perhaps, or a cockerel. A few enterprising children subsist by selling rats, mice, and pigeons. My specialty was pigeons. I hunted them after dark when they would not take flight. What I couldn't sell I ate, because when I begged for food or coin I received white robes, instead.

The hecatomb has been happening for all of recorded history, but no one seems to know why. Although I went to the library as many times as permitted (once every three years, and no more), no librarian would tell me anything about it other than it must be observed, *or else*. I remember the tomes and

scrolls chained like prisoners. I don't know what secrets lay within. When I asked to be taught to read, I was shooed away. No one would tell me anything at the temples, either, where augurs gazed at the sky for a sign.

The Butcher of Mazdin stands in front of the ruined palace in the centre of the city. With his cleaver held aloft and his empty eyes staring down at the crumbling, vine-choked ramparts, he is a foreboding sight. No bird dares roost atop this bronze giant. Not even a pigeon, though their flocks fill the sky most days. The augurs tell us it is notable that birds do not roost atop the Butcher's head. It is portentous, they say, but I do not know why. He gleams so bright in the sun that when I look away, it leaves shimmering holes in my vision.

As the solstice nears, people grow restless. Although nothing is dead yet, kettling vultures circle the city. The pigeons have all flown away. When the vultures land in the square, their gawky bald heads dip up and down just like the augurs. Augurs won't buy pigeons from the likes of me. My birds are too common. I am too poor, and they don't want to see my bad leg. They tend their own in gilded coops, breeding fancy ones with curly plumage or feathered feet. Augurs raise and lower their heads like the vultures do. They mark observations down before chaining the scrolls like prisoners in the library.

Just before the square fills with people and their sacrifices, vultures run along the streets, necks outstretched, wings flapping. They lurch back into the sky before filling the trees. Their eyes track the parade of people and animals entering the square, and I wonder how many sacrifices they've attended. There's a saying that you are what you eat. Since vultures feast after every hecatomb, perhaps they are made of reborn souls. As for me, I am a pigeon. I am stolen bread. I am garbage.

One day I snuck into a shop filled with wondrous things. Pots of strange salves and unguents, thin-necked pots reeking of camphor and sulphur, solid iron rings which could be joined together and taken apart again, cotton gauze which erupted in flame before vanishing as though it never existed. The purveyor was a magician. He used doves instead of pigeons. Let them vanish and reappear. Such a place was not for the likes of me, but I went in anyway. When the shopkeep wasn't looking, I pocketed a knife. He never saw me enter. He never saw me leave. I have my own kind of magic. Unless we're in the way, paupers are invisible to those who do not wish to see us. Eyes slide over us. People look away, especially when we are lame.

No animal accompanies me this time as I limp my way to the Butcher of Mazdin. Despite the bad leg which makes people's eyes slide past me, my lack of sacrificial victim makes me conspicuous. The beady eyes of birds bore into me. Congregants stare, and at first, they look confused, but that soon turns to rage and terror. If anyone refuses to make a blood sacrifice, the *or else* will happen. The ire of the congregants makes my heart beat too quickly. I'm not used to being noticed. My hands tremble and my knees begin to buckle beneath my white charity robe, but I am determined.

At my first ceremony fourteen years ago, back when my leg was still good, I'd brought a white pigeon mottled with grey. I'd crept along the rooftops the night before and caught her in her nest. I stuffed her in a bag and sucked her two eggs dry while her mate buffeted me with his wings. I left him behind and slept beneath a bush with his wife in the bag next to my head. In the queue to the square the next morning, a rich benefactor handed me my robe. I pulled it over my patched rags. It was too big because I was too thin. Beneath the blinding white sun of the hecatomb, I opened my bag and the piebald pigeon fluttered in my hands until I stopped her for good. I tried to lay her gently in the pile, but no gentleness was to be had. Screams of the dying and the soon-to-die filled the air. Made my ears ring. Gore lapped at my legs. Spattered my face and arms. My gifted robe could never be white again.

One of the victims wasn't dead. A mouse skittered out from between twitching corpses. This tiny creature swam through a gutter running high with stinking blood, its little nose peeking out from the red, its coat caked and clotted, whiskers glistening in the dazzle of the noonday sun. This secret survivor scuttled up the Butcher of Mazdin's leg and vanished. Though I clambered over the heap and around the monument in my ruined robe, I couldn't find where it went.

That next year, we experienced a plague of mice. Rodents overran all of Mazdin, devouring the best of all foods, and I heard it said that no cat caught even a single mouse that year. The augurs had theories about this, but so did everyone. No one mentioned seeing a mouse run up the Butcher's leg. Perhaps I alone had witnessed it.

Seven years ago, I brought another pigeon with feathers shining like hematite to the sacrifice. He was the last pigeon I ever caught. I'd found him sleeping on a shelf beneath a stone bridge, helpless in the pre-dawn gloom. At the hecatomb, he stared up at me with bright orange eyes lidded like a setting sun between dark clouds. I wrenched his head from his fluttering body with my bare hands and flung the carcass onto the heap.

That was the year a princess had outdone herself by giving thousands of white robes to all the city's poor. This act left the other nobles grumbling, arms holding white robes which would be worn by no one. The princess was determined to outshine everyone. Maybe even the Butcher himself. The other nobles brought cattle. Pure white heifers without blemish. She brought a bull elephant, his tusks tipped with gold and studded with rubies.

The elephant was a menace, trumpeting in fear and goring with his tusks. Rampaging through the streets, he made a few sacrifices of his own. At one point, he reared up on his hind legs, towering over the growing pile of bodies just as the Butcher of Mazdin towered over the rest of us. The elephant trampled many before being brought down by the guards. Three rich people died. No one counted the paupers who died.

I survived, though my leg hasn't been the same since. There would be no more hunting pigeons for me. While I lay screaming, I saw, or perhaps I hallucinated, a macaque making its way out of the pile of corpses and up the red-streaked leg of the Butcher of Mazdin. The monkey disappeared into a dazzle of sunlight.

That year, macaques overran Mazdin. Little monkeys with long tails and serious faces pelted people with fruit and faeces. Little monkeys cavorted through the streets, taking whatever they wanted whenever they wanted. Not a single monkey was caught that whole year. Not a single monkey was stopped. Every macaque was sleek and fat and happy, and I too wanted to be sleek and fat and happy.

Both my blood and the blood of sacrifices have crimsoned my robes and run through the gutters. This year, however, it won't be an animal who scales the Butcher of Mazdin. While others glare at me, I draw the little dagger I stole from the magic shop. As I plunge it into my chest, the trick blade disappears into the hilt. It falls onto the ground when I collapse onto the growing pile of sacrifices. An offering is an offering, and though human sacrifices are rare, they aren't unheard of. Besides, I am a pauper. I am invisible. My eyes are shut as I play dead in my charity robes. The bodies pile atop me, and I am forgotten. When the congregants leave and vultures descend upon the feast, I begin to wriggle my way out. It takes me a long time, and the stink is fierce. The bodies are heavy and lay atop me like cold, heaped clay, but the vultures help. They pull and pluck at the corpses, and I can finally squirm my way free, leaving my gore-soaked robe behind. They hop clear when they see me, but when I don't bother them, they go back to their banquet.

The pedestal upon which the Butcher of Mazdin stands is high, but the heap of bodies is high, too, and even with my twisted leg, I am able to climb it. Above me is an aperture just big enough to squeeze into. I pull myself inside. No one but the vultures see. The Butcher of Mazdin is hollow and filled with light.

I look upwards. Ever upwards. I ignore the bones of the mouse. Ignore the bones of the macaque. Ignore the bones I do not recognize. The sun pours in through the Butcher's empty eyes. I use my nails to pull myself up, all the way to roost inside his miraculous head. I pray that next year will be a good year for paupers, and maybe for pigeons, too.

Shantell Powell is a swamp hag, Indigiqueer, and elder goth raised in an apocalyptic cult on the land and off the grid. She's a graduate of the Writers' Studio at Simon Fraser University and the Banff Centre for Arts and Creativity's horror residency. A Brave New Weird winner, an Aurora finalist, and a Journey, Best of the Net, and Pushcart nominee, her writing is in Augur Magazine, The Deadlands, On Spec, and more. When she's not writing, she wrangles chinchillas and gets filthy in the woods.

Sound Trails

Art by Vesqid

I Dumped My Girlfriend: Black Dresses' *LAUGHINGFISH*

By
Dorian Bowser

2020 was a mindbreaking year for listeners of the lesbian electronic slash noise pop band from Toronto, Black Dresses, as the duo announced their breakup with the debut of their final album *PEACEFUL AS HELL*. Due to a punishing culmination of pressures that I could only describe as "2020", Black Dresses as a band would no longer exist. *PEACEFUL AS HELL* was a final sharp nail hammered into the duo's coffin lid. And the Dead Girls of Black Dresses would stay dead and buried—at least, until Valentine's Day 2021. The resurrection that was *FOREVER IN YOUR HEART* is considered by some to be the duo's magnum opus; Devi McCallion's beautiful yet eerie lyrics served to once again viciously complement Ada Rook's cutesy yet grinding vocals. They created a mixture of heightened emotions and revitalized love, death, suffering, overcoming. Black Dresses' albums tend to begin with devastating and personal spiels of guilt, pain, or emptiness before culminating in a final hopeful cry for love and peace. After all, Black Dresses started as a demo project between two struggling strangers who met across the interwebs, only to morph into a manifestation of the love that blossomed between the duo who found a home in each other.

And *LAUGHINGFISH*, the 2024 double-LP, murdered Black Dresses in cold blood.

"This is like their third 'final' album, so I doubt this is it honestly," says a reddit comment posted the day the project fell to Earth.

LAUGHINGFISH was first teased rather joyfully, on the podcast episode "Amazing Ape 2016 feat. Black Dresses" by Boys Bible Study. But the album evolved into a monster—*LAUGHINGFISH* is the daughter of the foul-smelling grime that ferments within romantic struggle. As an art piece, it serves as a fascinating case study of dying love, and toxic codependence; the mortality of the love between Rook and Devi.

"I DUMPED MY GIRLFRIEND," posted Devi on her Instagram story.

"This is the last one," Rook tweeted, unusually solemn.

Devi claimed that the theme of the album was "is having a bad childhood an excuse for having a bad adulthood?".

Rook stated that this was simply not true—that Devi could only speak on the parts of the album that she wrote.

With a twinge of bitter salt, Devi would mention that the initial idea behind the album was actually a "breakup concept album" suggested by Rook—to drag the feelings out in art, without the actuality of them. General themes of the album revolve around codependency, monotony, and exhaustion.

The album opens with "FANTA", which starts the album with hushed whispers, and low, vibrating synths. Its tone is ominous, and a frightened uncertainty twinkles. Lyrics within *LAUGHINGFISH* toy with a metaphorical tale of two sisters, writhing in a grief-stricken and broken life. Their relationship spirals in an abusive, dependent circle that borders on dangerous, and incestuous. But slivers of the singers' real lives seep between the lines. Familiar tales from Rook's solo albums, *2020 Knives* and *Shed Blood*, echo amongst the facade of fictional sickened sisterhood.

The first and only song from *LAUGHINGFISH* to drop as a single, "BAD VEGGIES", is much more brash than the opening track. It opens with aggressive tones, reminiscent of a rather scratchy nuclear alarm siren. Lyrics by both Rook and Devi are delivered in a tone that's much more panicked, there's a dire need to get these feelings out from where they're buried in their chests. A much more abrasive song, it attacks the theme of misery or even abuse much harder, even with just its instrumental noise. Both singers mix grating screams into their parts. "Push her down into the marble floor," Devi chokes. Even between these hints of anguish, the song concludes with a beg from Rook, "I can't do this on my own, I need you, *please*." The dire need is replaced with a dire plea.

"WOUNDED ANIMAL" follows up with more quiet melodies, softer chords. Differing from "FANTA", the piece lacks an edge of fear. The song is more reflective of the past, reflecting on change, reflecting on where we've come. A rather personal verse from Rook details her past lives, her past mistakes, and her past homes over the years. "...Got a band out there, maybe things will change" especially invokes a yearning for what Black Dresses would bring—despite the melancholy that it encompasses in its end.

But the showstopping track of *LAUGHINGFISH*, "IF YOU FIND ME GONE", serves to once again slaughter any optimistic hints that may have escaped in the buildup to it. It's more of a spoken-word poem than a song but instigates the deepest sorrows of the album thus far despite its lack of diverse sound. Devi's lyrics grapple with suicidal ideation, while Rook's lyrics toy with panic over losing her safe space despite hinting at destructive fights between the two of them. The song reeks of death in a more obvious way than the others have thus far, reminiscent of more horror movie-like songs in their previous albums such as *THANK YOU*. For those familiar with the duo, some verses send uneasy shivers down your vertebrae. It leaves you wondering which parts of *LAUGHINGFISH* are purely conceptual, or which parts are reminiscent of their break. The song is monotonous and hollow in many aspects, relatively unlayered and empty of noises compared to previous songs from the duo, but this only contributes to its hard-hitting depth when contrasted with the spectacular writing.

"CAN'T KEEP THE KNOTS OUT" with its deep bouncing tones, opens with a similar bleak monotony that's especially emphasized by Devi's first set of lyrics—"I laughed at you in your lowest low… No I won't cut your hair, but I can't keep the knots out," she sings dark notes from her stomach. The song is reminiscent of depressive slumps and the consequences of lashing out. But it's punchy and electric, with an almost videogame-like mixing. The verses revolve around and amplify each other as the story builds. "I think I liked you better still alive" calls back to the solidarity that these dead girls once had, in albums like *LOVE AND AFFECTION FOR STUPID LITTLE BITCHES*. "Dead girls dry each other's eyes and pretend for a while that we're still alive" was sung by Rook and Devi together, years ago.

"IT'S PROBABLY FINE" directly follows the previous track and continues its imagery. "It's probably fine," sings Devi, "what do I get if I change? I'll never change, I'll stay ashamed" is very much representative of feeling trapped in your current life, stuck in a situation that feels like it's draining you. Healing, escaping it, is only a distant fantasy. "It's in your head, It's paranoid, It's your fantasy, It's suicide… I'm sure it's probably fine". The repetitive arrangement emphasizes the perpetual cycle of wanting to improve, wanting to escape, wanting to wallow in it forever, wanting to end it, and remaining motionless, moving neither up or down, despite it all. The ending of the song drags out with Rook's grunts of pain, and a stinging harsh note.

The final track, "THE SILENCE", has a much more upbeat style that's more reminiscent of other Black Dresses finale tracks, that tended to close the albums with a hopeful, or thankful conclusion. Despite *LAUGHINGFISH*'s birth as a child of divorce, "THE SILENCE" plays like a piece that was written with love, with Rook and Devi laughing and giggling alongside each other as the final album comes to a close. But there's still a mournful undertone to the last track, particularly as Devi sings nonchalantly, "no one was there to take me home". To "emerge from a state of silence" may seem like a positive note to leave on, but the line is more of a double-edged sword, as to emerge from a state of silence is to enter one of chaos, noise, and pain. It's going to hurt.

22 individual tracks, 1 hour and 17 minutes, the extended length of the album drags out the depressive spiral in a way that contributes to the heavy cloud it puts over the head of the listener. And I say this in an affectionate way—although leaving me with a rather sinking feeling in my chest, *LAUGHINGFISH* accomplishes its goal(?) of *making it hurt*. And it leaves a fantastically vibrant pain, a nostalgic aching need for joy. Publicized reviews of *LAUGHINGFISH* remark that the project is simply just too long—too convoluted, or even just demo-quality. But from the perspective of a long-time Black Dresses fan (even though I would probably rather be listening to *PEACEFUL AS HELL* as I walk to organic chemistry lab at 8 in the morning), *LAUGHINGFISH* is a beautiful yet tragically violent end to the band.

"When God flooded the earth, the fish laughed," said Devi.

Dorian is a senior in the honors college at Oregon State University, majoring in biology. They have a profound interest in Metal Gear Solid, the dorid nudibranch *Rostanga pulchra,* and the music work of Ada Rook. Between research and schooling they make art, zines, and write as a hobby– so they are very pleased to be able to write for the first volume of SLUGGER! :)

Season of the Witch Review

By
Nico Bell

Peter Bebergal delves into the depts of occultism and rock and roll in his meticulously researched book *Season of the Witch: How the Occult Saved Rock and Roll.* From the early origins of the blues to the contemporary music of Madonna, mysticism and the supernatural are woven seamlessly into the vast history and uprising of one of music's bedrock genres.

While presenting readers with a wealth of precise analytics to back up his research, Bebergal dares readers to expand their minds and shift away from a "one size fits all" definition of occultism. He turns back time and dips readers into Greek mythology, exploring the influence of Pan—a horned deity who encourages nature, community, and universal understanding—while also exploring various more modern definitions related such as paganism, magic, and wicca.

As the narrative settles in, most chapters are spent volleying heavily between the 60s and 70s while exploring themes of racism, religion, and drugs. Whether readers tumble down the rabbit hole of Syd Barrett's LSD psychedelic trips, listen to the crackle of sin-laced albums burning in bonfires at the hands of fearful Christians, or hear the accusations of white critiques claiming Jay-Z's successes is solely achieved from a connection to the Illuminati, Bebergal offers readers well-paced viewpoints exploring mysticism.

There are some notable historical music moments left out, but it's made up for by a wealth of iconic artists: Pink Floyd, The Beatles, Rolling Stones, Black Sabbath, Led Zeppelin, Alice Cooper, David Bowie, Death Metal, Kiss, Madonna, Robert Moog, and Jay-Z. Perhaps some readers may desire more pages dedicated to later years such as the 1980s satanic panic or artists in the early 2000s, but overall, it's an engaging look at the occult's influence on one of the most controversial genres throughout time. Readers who enjoyed *Aleister Crowley: Magick, Rock and Roll, and the Wickedest Man in the World* by Gary Lachman or *The Occult Elvis: The Mystical and Magical Life of the King* by Miguel Conner will rock out to Bebergal's dizzying trip down rock and roll's vast legacy.

Nico Bell is the author of This Cruise Sucks and Gobble 'Til You Wobble: A New Year's Eve Nightmare. She is also the Editor-in-Chief at Mad Axe Media. When she isn't writing, she can be found playing with her very energetic dog, Egg. You can find her on Insta and TikTok @nicobellfiction or on her website www.nicobellfiction.com

Gen Z Turns to Folk

By
C. P. Bearden

If your algorithm is anything like mine, you've probably been inundated with videos of kids playing bluesy folk songs on acoustic guitars against a backdrop of green fields or tranquil forests. These shaggy-haired indie artists have been sprouting up like weeds this year in a trend that has some music critics scratching their heads.

For most of the twenty-first century, the trajectory of pop music was to get louder and more extravagant. Technological advancements in sound recording pushed the limits of what was possible, and there was no shortage of artists eager to leave their mark on the industry. Electronic music dominated the landscape with thumping beats, and even rock and metal bands added software instruments to their mixes, making their drums and guitars even more massive than they already were.

But it looks as though the next generation of musicians is yearning for music that calls back to a simpler time. Enter: The indie folk wave of 2025.

Nowadays it seems like everyone with a guitar and a Focusrite audio interface is posting their recordings on TikTok or Instagram. The songs are quiet when compared to most modern music, with relatable choruses and a distinctive lo-fi sound. Sometimes the lyrics are overtly political; other times they bemoan the struggles of modern life in a more general sense. The songs often don't feature any drums, and if they do, they're often subdued.

One of my favorite players in this new musical era is Hudson Freeman. He recently unveiled his song "If You Know Me" after clips of it went viral on social media. Within a month of its release, the song garnered over a million plays on Spotify. It has an unmistakable, raw quality to it and was clearly recorded outdoors, something that just doesn't happen in other genres. You can even hear a car revving its engine in the background. I wouldn't be surprised if Hudson opted to keep this take—one most artists would scrap—because it gives the song an authentic feel.

In this way, Hudson and others like him are rejecting the notion that music should (or even can) be perfect. They don't try to hide mistakes or hiccups in their songs, because to them, the flaws are what give their songs character. There's a kind of punk DIY ethos to it all that's refreshing after years of glitz and glam being force-fed to us by our algorithms.

With the rise of AI, this gritty authenticity stands as a reminder of the human element that makes music so special. It's always been the cornerstone of art in every form.

Even the aesthetic of these new artists is its own rejection of modern perfectionism culture. Thrift store clothes and faces without makeup are what you'll find in clips of musicians who in every way seem like ordinary people.

If you find yourself wondering why folk music is making a comeback now, all you need to do is look at the current state of affairs in the world.

To call 2025 a tumultuous year would be the understatement of the century. With widening income inequality and a political class that makes dystopian fiction feel quaint, things are looking more and more bleak for America's youth. Add to this a pandemic of isolation fueled by the very tech that was supposed to bring us together, and you have all the ingredients for the current indie folk revival.

Those of us who have been around the block a few times will recall that when the going gets tough, the people turn to folk. This wave isn't the first one, and it surely won't be the last. The genre's inherent anti-establishment qualities come as a respite to young people who are feeling more pessimistic about the future than ever.

So it's no surprise to see so many Zoomers today abandoning their MIDI keyboards and electric guitars in favor of acoustic ones. Similar folk waves have popped up in a cycle dating back to the Cold War.

In essence, folk is the pulse of America's music scene. Sometimes it's more prominent than at others, but it's never truly dead, and I suspect it never will die. It's the anthem of the downtrodden masses, the siren song of a rising generation.

And by the looks of things, it's not going anywhere.

C. P. Bearden is a musician, poet, and author. He's been involved in the punk and hardcore music scenes since he was a teenager, playing in multiple bands over the years. These days he spends his time begging other bands to come play in the small Georgia town he calls home.

Content Notes

A Cat Walked Across the Keyboard by Michael Bettendorf
- Drugs/overdosing

Hot Tub Hormone Xenotransfusion by L. Sanguine
- Dysphoria, transphobia, vomiting, physical violence

The Other Man by Kareem Miskel
- N/A

Contractual by P.L. McMillian
- N/A

Happy Hour at Harry's Hole in the Wall by Joshua Dobson
- N/A

Snuff by Madeline White
- Graphic description of a woman miscarrying a deformed, nonviable fetus. General background of misogyny and substance use. Discussion of nuclear apocalypse.

My Correspondence with the Goat Man by Jon Clendaniel
- N/A

Thin Man by e rathke
- N/A

The Money Left in the Account by Jennifer Jeanne McArdle
- Suicide, sibling death

The Butcher of Mazdin by Shantell Powell
- Blood sacrifice, harm to animals

Meet the Staff

Sam Logan, Co-Founding Editor

Sam Logan (he/him) emerged in 1984 from the depths of the Chesapeake Bay off the Maryland shore. He made it to Oregon where he is a university professor in kinesiology and teaches courses about punk, body horror, and Taylor Swift. Sam lives with his partner, kiddo, and Dune the dog. He has stories in Mouthfeel Fiction, Punk Noir Magazine, Divinations Magazine, Major 7th Magazine, Creepy Pod, and Wallstrait, among others. His story "Belly Bees" earned 9th place in the 2024 TL;DR 2k terrors competition. Find him at samloganwrites.com.

Arwyn Sherman, Co-Founding Editor

Arwyn Sherman lives in the woods of Maine with a menagerie of animals, including a chronically ill ferret. Their work has appeared in anthologies, on a few stages, and is probably tucked away in a chapbook you forgot you bought at a late night poetry show. Their debut, We, the Missing, will be released in May 2026 from Conquest Publishing. For more of them, visit www.arwynsherman.com/

Cover Artist, Kae Ranck

Kae Ranck is a freelance artist and writer currently slugging their way through life with their two cats. They graduated from Oregon State University in 2025 with a degree in Art and, as all art majors do, is now seeking out a JD at the University of Kansas. When not hunched over a desk like a shrimp to work, Kae can be found communing with plants and listening to niche 80s music like The Cramps.

Interior Layout & Formatter, Leo Otherland

A literal goblin masquerading as human, Leo Otherland is a queer member of the SFWA, weaver of delightfully soul-shattering speculative fiction, and lover of all things strange and unordinary. This elusive scribbler acquired his passion for weaving stories of dark and broken things through a childhood spent huddling in books and dodging the unfriendly spirits that resided in the haunted house they called home. Hidden somewhere unobtrusive in the arctic north woods of Wisconsin, Leo continually doodles several projects at once, while reading innumerable books and somehow keeping all the plotlines straight. During the few occasions it is not otherwise occupied, this finicky, unrepentant otaku enjoys reading web comics, watching anime, and playing JRPGs. While it's rare to catch this skittish wordsmith out in daylight, Leo can occasionally be located on his website, leootherland.com, or on various social media @LeoOtherland.

Interior Artists

Kit Carter works in both traditional and digital art, with a current focus on the latter. A recently discovered foreign entity known as 'free time' is now being used to feverishly contribute to a long-neglected artistic hobby, since Kit just recently graduated from Oregon State University in 2025 with a degree in psychology. Find Kit on Instagram @kvac_createscv

Born from the foggy oasis of the Pacific Northwest, Mike David was born with a pencil fused into his hand. As he got older, doctors surgically removed it, but he got used to the feeling and hasn't put it down since. Mike enjoys traditional art more than digital, so if you see any pencil lines underneath the line art, no you didn't. Mike currently resides in Corvallis, OR... for now...

Vesqid (he/him) is a queer artist and a second-year student at Oregon State University, studying nuclear engineering. Along with drawing recreationally, he also writes genre-inspired fiction.

Emma Fujikawa is an Oregon State University student majoring in graphic design. She hails from Kailua, Hawaii and became interested in art during quarantine. When she has free time, she also enjoys reading and playing casual soccer.

Esme (she/her) is an art student always looking for new fun ways to create weird stuff. If you're interested in watching her progress, you can follow her Instagram account: @esmekiddie